NANA BELLE WINS THE LOTTERY

TETER KEYES

*To my brothers Dave and Jim, and my grandsons, Zachary
and Roy III. Over the years, they have allowed me to observe
the fascinating workings inside the brains of ten- and eleven-
year-old boys. Love you guys.*

ACKNOWLEDGMENTS

Many thanks to my writer friends. Your input helped me shape the work and smooth the rough spots. As always, thank you to my daughters, Cher and Chasta, and my grandchildren for supporting my writing habit. Thank you to Joe, chief driver on our research trip to the Carolinas.

CHAPTER ONE

Mom is pinching the skin between her eyebrows. It's a totally familiar thing. What normally follows is, "Henry, to your room. Now." When that happens, I claim innocence, but I usually know the reason she's angry. This time I am innocent and whoever is on the other end of their phone conversation is the one in deep doo-doo.

"Are you sure?" she is saying. Pinch, pinch. "Calm down. Just tell me what happened."

The caller is one of my grandmothers. I know this because she said, "Hi, Mom," when she answered. What I don't know is whether it is Nana Belle, her mother, or Grandma Grace, Dad's mom.

"What, what?" I ask her, bouncing on my toes.

Mom waves me away and turns her back to me, listening. Pond scum, I'm ten years old and still being treated like a baby.

"Okay, okay," Mom is saying. "Did you talk to anyone about this yet?"

Silently, she listens.

"No, I don't mean Rita and Mary Beth. I mean someone at their office. At least talk to a lawyer before you–" She stops talking, listens again.

Rita and Mary Beth are my aunts, Mom's sisters, so I now know it must be Nana Belle on the phone.

Bounce, bounce.

Mom turns back around and points at my feet. I try to stop bouncing. It's hard.

My grandpa, John McNally, died before I was born, and Mom asked Nana if she has already talked to my aunts, so that means no one has died. That leaves someone is sick, there's been a fire, or a sinkhole opened up under Nana Belle's old Nebraska house. Dad says I have a calculating mind. He claims credit for that since he writes complicated software and says it requires serious machinations. Mom says I'm just a Curious George, like in the book she used to read to me, and that all my curiosity will get me in trouble one day, just like George.

I'd like to watch a big sinkhole swallow a house. Not with Nana Belle inside, of course. I picture a deep, round hole gobbling up Nana's home. I imagine the panicked squeal of her squeaky screen door as the old porch is sucked down.

Mom pushes the button to end the call and drops onto a chair. She pulls her hair back with both hands like she's trying to keep the top of her head from popping off.

"What, what?" I ask again, bouncing on my feet.

"I gotta call your dad," she says and stands up.

"Mom!" I shout. "Did Nana Belle's house fall into a sinkhole?"

"A what?"

Oops, imagination overflow.

She looks at me, puzzled. I take a big breath and ask as calmly as I can, "What did Nana say?"

She put her hands on my shoulders. Her eyes are all shiny. "Henry, your nana just won the lottery."

My turn to ask, "What?"

"The Powerball. The big one. Nana won it." She twirls around the room, singing, "Momma won it. One hundred and nine million smackers. She won, she won. One hundred and nine million. I can't believe it."

She stops mid-twirl and puts a hand over her mouth. Around it, she says, "I gotta call your dad." Then she picks up her phone and goes outside.

The lottery? This is better than watching Nana's house flush down a hole.

I didn't think all the twirling was just happiness for my nana. I'm guessing Mom believes some of that money will come to her and my aunties.

And aren't I the only child of loving parents? Snap, I am. Visions of new gaming systems and the upcoming new video game I saw on TV dance in my head.

The next two days are busy. Mom acts all weird. She made a jillion, million calls to my nana and aunties. She takes my old clothes out of drawers and closets, the ones I already grew out of, but then she gets all distracted and the piles sit on my floor for a couple of days. Once she was fixing supper, and the chicken almost burned because she kept on staring out the window. She and Dad have conversations in their room with the door shut. Hello, did you forget you had a kid?

"Mom?" I keep asking, but she just pats me on the back and says things will all work out. Zombieville.

Mom gets tickets so we can fly out to visit Nana Belle. I want Dad to come with us. Mom does too, but he tells Mom he loves her, but there was no way he is going to spend time with her family.

They talk in whispers in the kitchen while I'm a room away with my earphones on. I don't have music playing, but they don't know that. Curious George I am, but how else can I know what's going on? Dad says "dysfunctional" in a loud whisper. I peek around the edge of my door and see Mom turning to him with the knife she had been using to chop tomatoes and she asks him if he wants to say that again. Apparently, Dad does not because he leaves.

"What're you listening to, Henry?" he asks when he walks past and pats my head.

"Just some music," I tell him. "Why don't you want to come with us?"

We had gone to Nebraska where Nana Belle lives two Christmases ago. What I remember is that everything was brown and dead-looking, and when I stood outside all I saw was sky in every direction. That is if anyone wanted to stay outside long enough in the cold and wind. It's totally different from Seattle where we live. I'm not even mentioning having to see my bratty girl cousins. No, I'm not looking forward to Nebraska.

"Mom," I ask over dinner, "Why can't I stay with Dad, and you go? It's cold at Nana's and Heather's a brat."

"Don't call Heather a brat," Mom said. "Plus, it's summer now."

Then what she says changes everything. "We're not going to Nebraska, anyway, honey. Nana rented a beach cottage on one of the islands off the South Carolina coast."

"Island? You mean with an ocean and boats and swimming and everything?" This is good news.

"That's right." Mom beams me a smile. "It's on the Atlantic Ocean, not the Pacific like Seattle. There'll be sandy beaches, and you can swim. But, young man," she continues, pointing a fork at me, "you will not swim without an adult present."

"Will Heather and Sarah Beth be there?"

"I think it's just going to be us, your aunts, and Nana, at least for now."

This is even better news.

She looks at me for a long time as if seeing how much I have grown. I straighten in the chair to make myself look taller. Then she tells my dad, "I hate to admit it, but you're right, my family is not a normal, healthy one."

Dad snorts.

"Things were, I'd guess you could say, difficult growing up, especially for Rita and Mary Beth. They're older than me. My dad, your Grandpa John, had problems."

"He was a drunk," Dad says.

"Hush, Peter. My dad was in the war, and he didn't come back the same. Now, he would have been diagnosed with PTSD, that's post-traumatic stress disorder," she explains to me. "Back then it was different; people didn't understand the condition. Plus, the vets coming back were criticized, some were even spat on."

She points a fork at my dad.

What is it with her today with the sharp stuff?

"He was still a successful man. He operated his pharmacy and provided for Mom and us. It's just that—"

"He drank," Dad says. "To excess. Often."

"Hello, I was there. I know he did, and it made home life difficult. Especially when my mother was—"

"An enabler," finishes my dad.

"Well, he had cut back a lot by the time I was in junior high. Life was easier then."

"Because he had cirrhosis of the liver. Not that it stopped him."

"Enough!"

"Anyway," she goes on, looking at me, "Your Nana Belle wants to get us girls together for a couple of weeks, see if we can talk things over, and find a way to come closer. We all suffered as kids, then we scattered across the country, and no one discussed it. Now with the money, there's an opportunity to get together, talk, and heal."

CHAPTER TWO

WEDNESDAY MORNING WE GET ON A PLANE TO SOUTH
Carolina. Mom's a teacher, and it's July, so she's free.
Me, too.

We change planes in Denver. Mom's already told
me it will be a long flight and packed snacks. I'm
making a list of things I want to buy in the notebook I
always carry with me when I hear my mom sniffle. She
pulls her purse out from under the seat, digs for a tissue, and wipes her eyes and nose.

"You okay, Mom?"

"Sure, honey, just thinking about things. The cabin
air must be too dry."

We're quiet for a while. Me working on my list and
Mom reading her Kindle.

"Mom?"

"Yes?"

I whisper, "You think Nana is going to give you
some of the money she won?"

"Yes," she whispers back. "She already told us she
wants to give us a share."

I lean in close. "Does that mean I get a bigger al-
lowance?"

Mom laughs and hugs me. "We'll see, young man. Don't think I haven't seen you working on your wish list."

Finally, we land. While we wait for our luggage, Mom talks on the phone. I look around, but all I see are people talking on phones or waiting. The carousel finally jerks awake, and Mom clicks off the phone. She's frowning.

"Is Nana Belle going to pick us up?" I ask.

"No. Apparently, Mary Beth is just too busy making dinner, and Nana isn't feeling well." She sighs then shakes her head. "Let's look for a cab that will take us to the ferry. It sounds like that's the only way to get to the island." She says something under her breath that I can't catch, picks up her suitcases, and we make our way to the door.

I do the same, except for the muttering.

A cab takes us to the harbor where we find the ferry. Last trip, the captain announces as we get on.

By the time we get off at the small dock on the island where Nana is staying, it's starting to get dark.

I'm starving. We had eaten at McDonald's when we switched planes in Denver and had snacks, but that seems like years ago. At least that's what my growling stomach claims.

We walk up the lighted path to the beach house Nana rented. I wonder what Aunt Mary Beth cooked for supper. Is it fried chicken, or maybe grilled? We walk a few more steps up the slope. Is it hamburgers with gobs of ketchup and fluffy white buns that have been smashed on top of the burgers while they're still in the pan? Yum.

Mom gives Nana a big hug.

"Mary Beth said you weren't feeling well, Mom. Are you okay?"

"Yes, honey," Nana tells my mom. "Just been tired is all with all the excitement and then the move here. Now you come here, young man, and give your nana a hug."

I do, breathing in the nana scent of flowers and baking bread.

It's Mary Beth's turn next. She hugs Mom, but it is a quick hug and release. My auntie is even fatter than the last time I saw her, and I'm glad she didn't swallow mom up in a bigger hug. She's wearing a baggy dress, and I see crooked toes on her bare feet. I wouldn't have noticed the toes except for the bright red toenail polish. She ruffles my hair but skips the hug. I sniff, still wondering about dinner.

"I wish you would have said something earlier," Mary Beth says. "Mom and I had TV dinners since it was just the two of us."

"Fried chicken," Nana says. "Mary Beth had two and then finished mine."

"Momma," Mary Beth says. "You said you weren't hungry. She pats her big belly. "I, on the other hand, was starving."

"Sure," Mom says, looking around. "Any of the frozen dinners left? We haven't had anything to eat since the Denver airport. I'm sure Henry's famished."

I nod big time.

"You can look, Jennifer," Nana says.

I sit down at the kitchen bar. Mom opens the freezer and rummages around.

"Rita will be here later," Nana says.

"Not if she's taking the ferry. We took the last one out for the day," Mom says, still searching. She pulls out a package, looks at it, and puts it back. "Don't you have anything other than fried chicken dinners?"

"I'm fine with that," I chime in.

"Nothing wrong with fried chicken and spuds," Mary Beth says. "Least it sticks to your ribs."

"I can tell," Mom says in that tone Dad and I know so well.

"Mom, chicken is fine with me," I say for the second time.

"Girls, I'm not going to have any bickering," Nana tells them. "I invited you all here, Rita too, because I want us to sit down and really talk with each other. God knows we had some difficult times when you were little."

"Dad drank and we all suffered, you mean," my mom says.

"Hush, don't speak badly of the dead. I know your dad had problems, but he still did well for us. We always had a roof over our heads and food on the table. That's better than some men I know. He worked hard and if he had a drink to relax, well—well, I just want us all to get along."

My mom goes over and hugs Nana. "Sorry, Mom. I think it's a great idea to get everyone together for a reunion. Thank you."

Nana sniffs, pulls a tissue from her pocket, and wipes her eyes. "I just thank God that I was blessed with the winning lottery ticket." She makes the sign of the cross—a touch to her forehead, stomach, left shoulder, right shoulder—then kisses her fingers and lifts them to the ceiling. I am surprised, considering I thought Nana was Methodist like us, but I don't say anything.

"It came just in time," she continues. "We've always owned the house, the one you girls grew up in, but I need to replace the roof. And the plumbing is bad. I haven't used the bathroom upstairs forever since the pipe under the vanity rotted out. Got tired of having to empty the bucket whenever I ran water in the sink."

"Mom, you should have said something. Peter and I would have paid to have a plumber come out and fix that."

"You have enough going on in your life, with teaching school and taking care of Henry. I didn't want to bother you."

Everyone turns to stare at me.

Awkward.

"I'm thinking of selling the old house, anyway," Nana continues. "I'm just rattling around in that big place, too much space. And the taxes and upkeep. That's the expensive part."

"But we all grew up in that home," Mary Beth says all whiney. "Think of all the memories we have there."

"So, you're saying your terrible childhood wasn't all that bad?" This from my mom in the sarcastic voice again. Two zingers in one day, a new record.

"How would you know anyway, Jennifer," Mary Beth shoots back. "You being the baby and all, growing up after Dad started Alcoholics Anonymous."

"Not that he ever took that seriously."

"Stop it," Nana says, slapping her hand on the countertop. "This is exactly what I was talking about. Bicker, bicker, that's all this family has done for years. I'm tired of it."

I keep my head down and go on eating the dinner Mom cooked in the microwave. This is interesting. Mom doesn't talk about being a kid other than to say she couldn't wait to go to college and get out of Nebraska. I pick up a chicken leg and chew on the bone. Mom watches, and then without me asking, pulls another dinner out of the freezer and puts it in the microwave. Mom's good at reading minds.

"I'm gonna fix up the house and sell it," Nana tells them. "Buy me a condo somewhere. A warm place on the beach, maybe. It's beautiful here, and I've always wanted to live near the ocean. Winters are pleasant, everyone says." She sighs, smiles. "I'm not going to miss snow at all." The smile widens. "Think I'll have enough money to get a little condo on the beach?"

Everyone laughs, and Nana grabs more hugs from us all.

The beach house Nana rented is big. In the great room are large windows and a sliding glass door that opens out to the beach. I step outside on the deck. There's a full moon, and the light makes the waves look like they're waving at the moon's face. I can see that the deck wraps all the way around the side of the house. This is going to be fun. I breathe in the warm salt air and then go back inside, holding a hand over my yawn.

"You're sleeping in the bedroom on that side," Nana says, pointing to a door.

The kitchen is open to the great room, and, on both sides, I see other doors leading to what looks like a bunch more rooms.

"There's a Jack and Jill bathroom between your room and the one on the other side." Nana points to a door near mine. "Jennifer, you can sleep in the room on the other side of the bathroom, next to Henry."

"I have the room closest to Mom," Mary Beth says smugly, and motions to the opposite corner. "Mom has the master, of course. There's a balcony off it, facing the sea." She looks at me for a moment and then says, "Jen, if I knew you were bringing Henry here, I would have brought my girls. But," she pauses, "I thought this was supposed to be a time for just Mom and us girls."

Inside I groan but manage to clamp it before the groan pops out.

"Peter's working on a big project," Mom explains. "He's been working ten to twelve hours a day."

"And what does he do again that's so all-fired important?" Mary Beth asks, one fist on a plump hip.

"Like I've explained to you before, Sis, his company writes software programs."

She waves the hand not on her hip. "That seems to be, I don't know, such a fuzzy science. At least my Stephen does something that we can visualize. He puts a 'For Sale' sign in front of a house, shows it to people, writes contracts, and then puts up a sold sign when the house sells. Real estate, that's something you can see, touch, feel."

"Touch and feel are the same," I say.

"You know what I mean, Henry," Mary Beth snaps. "Don't get smart."

Mom starts to say something back to her sister, but Nana Belle puts out a hand in a 'stop' gesture and gives a loud whistle. Go, Nana.

"This is exactly what I wanted to avoid," she says. Then speaking slowly and deliberately, "We are all going to have a nice visit, and we are going to get along."

Suddenly, I'm very tired. I grab a suitcase and go to my assigned room.

Five minutes later, I come back out.

"Nana, how do I connect with your Internet? You have a router set up?"

Nana looks puzzled for a moment then says, "No Internet out here, honey. And cell phones don't work this far from the mainland. All we have is the landline. When it works, that is. That's the number your mom called on earlier."

"No Internet?" I can't believe it. "I guess I'll just watch TV."

"No television reception either," Nana is smiling. I'm feeling doom.

"Sorry, honey," Nana went on. "That's one of the reasons I selected this place. No distractions. There's plenty to do. There are fishing poles in storage under the house. You can walk on the beach looking for shells, read, swim, snorkel. I think there are even a couple of bicycles around."

I'm so doomed, I think as I slump back to my room.

CHAPTER THREE

AUNT RITA IS IN THE KITCHEN THE NEXT MORNING WHEN I go for breakfast. Unlike Mary Beth, she looks the same way she did two years ago when we went to Nebraska for Christmas. She's as tall as my mom when she wears high heels, and she always wears them. Opposite of Aunt Mary Beth, she's skinny, and her face is all tight like her bones are about to pop through. This morning, she's talking fast and searching through the kitchen cabinets, just as fast.

"I can't believe it. My plane gets in late. Then I find out the damn ferry quits running at seven o'clock. Can you believe that?" She goes on before anyone has a chance to answer. "I even told the guy running the fuel pumps at the dock that I was willing to pay fifty bucks to get across the bay. But apparently, gas jockeys make so much money he could turn me down. Can you believe that?"

No one even tries to answer this time.

"I ended up having to get a motel room for the night, and then I caught the first ferry out. Where in the hell are the bowls? I need one for my yogurt."

"Up there." Nana points to a cabinet. I'm positive I saw Aunt Rita open it already.

"Then the motel charges me a fortune."

She suddenly stops, looks at Nana, and smiles.

"I guess we can afford that now, can't we, Mom? Have you hired an attorney to get, you know, things arranged yet? That's a lot of money. I hope it's someone we can trust."

Two things. My Aunt Rita, Margarita is her real name, but no one ever calls her that, is a lawyer in Chicago. Dad said she works for a firm that specializes in civil law, whatever that is. He told me it means that she rarely goes to court since the parties prefer to settle, and no one ever goes to jail. Second, I noticed she used the word "we" when she talked about the money Nana won.

"I'm sure Momma's already done that. Right, Momma?" Mary Beth asks.

"Yes, I already set up a trust," Nana Belle answers. "Stan Daniels helped me. He's been our family lawyer for years, and I trust him."

"Stan Daniels?" Rita squeaks. "What is he, a hundred years old by now? Hell, he was old and cranky when I was still in high school." She turns and glares at Nana, hands on hips. "You're playing in a whole new ballpark now, Mom. Daniels was competent for when Dad died, and we had to probate his estate. But that's nothing compared to now." She snorts. "Your game just got upped. A hundred million. Hell, it takes skill to work with that amount."

"It's a hundred and nine million," Mary Beth says.

"What?"

"Momma won a hundred and nine million, not a hundred."

Rita waves a hand, dismissing her sister. "A hundred, a hundred nine, what the flip. It's a damn lot of cash. Too much for some little country lawyer to sort through."

"Momma," Mary Beth says. "You do what you want with it. You know I love you and whatever you decide to do is fine." She pauses. "I know you love us, too, and you'll do what's best for your family, right?"

My mom joins us, hair still damp from the shower.

"Morning, Rita, glad you made it."

She kisses the top of my head. "Morning, sweetheart, you sleep well?"

"Yes," I say, "but I'm starving."

"You ate a ton last night, Henry, and you're still hungry?" Mary Beth huffs. "What is it with boys that age? All they think of is food."

"He's growing fast."

Go Mom. My aunt really can't complain since she obviously eats. A lot.

Mom finds the cereal and pours us each a bowl. "What's the plan for today, Mom? You said you wanted to get together and talk with us."

"Mom said old Stan Daniels set up a trust," Rita tells her, spooning yogurt into a bowl. "I'm wondering if the old coot is even competent to do something so complicated. We have skilled estate and trust attorneys in our Chicago office that I'm sure would be better. What does the trust say, anyway, Mom?"

Nana starts to answer, but Rita keeps on going. "And then there's the matter of money management. You'll want to invest so that the trust can grow and provide a suitable income for you. Are you saying Stan's going to do all that, too?"

Again, Nana starts to answer, but again, my aunt runs right over her.

"There're all kinds of cons out there that would be glad to assist," Rita's fingers make quote marks in the air when she says 'assist.' "And then poof, your money disappears along with the adviser. She makes quote marks around 'adviser,' too. "I can't tell you how many clients we have that this happened to."

"Clients who are victims, or who perpetrated the fraud?" asks my mom, all innocent-like.

Rita glares at Mom, but my mom is concentrating on pouring orange juice, so she doesn't see.

"All kinds. That's why I know how easily Mom can be separated from her winnings."

"Girls, stop, please," Nana says, putting her hands over her ears. "All this bickering has to stop. For God's sake, you're all adults now with your own lives, but here you are acting like children. When I'm gone, you three girls will be all the family that's left. I want you to love each other, spend holidays together, turn to each other for support."

"But, Momma, we're all very different," Mary Beth says.

"I know, honey. Rita's a successful lawyer. Jen teaches, that's an important job, and you," Nana turns to Mary Beth, "you have a busy life with your three daughters."

"And I help Stephen in his real estate business," Mary Beth huffs. "Plus, when the girls all get in school, I plan to finish my degree so I can work as an LPN."

"Yes," Nana says, drawing out the word, "and how is Stephen's business doing, anyway? He always tells me he's doing great but then again, you asked for—"

"What?" Rita jumps in. "Did you ask Mom for money already? After all the bragging Stevie does about the big deals he puts together?"

"His name is Stephen, I've told you that before, and we just asked for a little loan to tide us over. He has expenses, you know, and it's not like he has a regular paycheck. Sometimes we have to wait a while for his commissions to come through."

"Mom's right," my mom says. "We're family here.

We have a shared history. Even though some parts were difficult with Dad, we're all grown now and it's time to get past all that."

"You just tell us what you want to tell us, Momma," Mary Beth says.

Finally, no one is talking. I jump right in. "Mom, can I be excused so I can go outside?"

"You're excused, Henry. Put your dishes in the sink, first, and don't wander too far."

I stack my bowl and spoon in the sink and escape.

A wood-planked walk leads down the hill from the house to the beach. The sun is out now, and I can see sand between the scrubby grass and the ocean. Living in Seattle, I know about the Pacific Ocean, but the Atlantic is different. The water here is a blue-gray and makes soft waves that chase my bare feet. I play catch with the waves, chasing them toward the ocean and jumping over the line of shells that have clumped at the tide line. Then I run back, again leaping over the shells.

A dead jellyfish has washed up, the round clear body like a bubble. When I poke it with a stick, it doesn't move. I poke harder and the jelly inside it squishes to the side. Poke, squish. Poke, squish. Just to make sure it's dead.

The beach curves around the front of the house and ends at a thick bunch of trees. In it are palms with their narrow trunks topped with fan-like leaves: tall, twisty trees with hairy clumps of Spanish moss, low bushes, and vines like ropes that dangle off the trees toward the ground. I put my sandals on and push through the shrub and vines. The ground is thick with dead leaves and stuff.

I'm an explorer deep in the jungle. I'm stalking wild beasts, walking really quietly, and getting closer and closer to a spotted panther.

Overhead, something chatters, and I quickly back out, vines grabbing at my ankles.

Blood-sucking squirrels, that's what lurks overhead, I discover when a little gray creature jumps from branch to branch chattering a warning.

I walk along the forest edge, past the beach house, and discover a place where the shrubs aren't as thick. I look around to make sure no one is watching, and then step into the deep green shade. No blood-sucking squirrels here. Good. It's hard to walk; dead leaves and stuff hide feet-trapping roots. I hear skittering noises. Snakes? Giant people-eating bugs? Panthers? It's spooky and, except for the skittering, so quiet I can almost hear the trees breathe. Something bites my neck, and I slap at it. Creepola, it's a blood-sucking, vampire mosquito.

A dead tree leans against the trunk of another tree, like an invitation. I climb the dead trunk to one wide branch and then swing up to another. After climbing for a while, the branches thin out, and I can see the roof of Nana's house. The flat ocean stretches into forever.

I know the earth curves away, cutting off the view, but I learned in school that ancient sailors believed the sea fell off the edge of the world and into space. That's much more interesting. I'm so high in the tree that it's like being in the crow's nest of a ship. I put the edge of one hand to my forehead and scan the horizon, looking for the sea monsters that lurk at the edge of the world. If only I had binoculars. A breeze stirs and the branches sway and creak.

A hammering sound comes from beyond the trees. Not squirrels. I swing up to a higher branch, and another one. Just past the forest, on the other side of the island, I can just see what looks like another roof. I stretch out an arm toward a branch so I can climb a little higher.

A whistle splits the quiet and birds scatter.

Monkey poop, it's Mom.

"Henry, Henry, where are you?" Another whistle. No one whistles louder than my mom, not even Dad.

I climb down as fast as I can. Only when my feet touch the ground do I yell back. "Here, Mom."

I'm not an A student for nothing. If my mom knew I had been climbing trees, she'd make me stop, and I'd never learn what lies on the other side of the island.

"Where have you been, young man?" Mom asks as I round the corner of the house.

"Exploring."

"Where?"

I pointed to the jungle of trees. "There."

She squints, sweeps her eyes from where the line starts near the sea to where it disappears behind the beach house. "Looks pretty thick in there, kiddo. Easy to get lost if you go through it, and who knows what kind of animals lurk inside."

"Panthers?" I ask. Now that would be fun.

She laughs. "No, I'm thinking poison ivy and snakes. I don't think we're in panther country."

"Vampire squirrels?"

"Henry James Rowley, you have quite an imagination. Just keep close, so I know where you are, okay?"

"Okay," I sigh, and she ruffles my hair.

"I'm going to put on my swimsuit and go for a swim. Want to join me?"

I do.

Supper is hot dogs and steak grilled over a fire set in a stone ring in the sand dunes below the house. I have both hot dogs and steak along with Mom's special potato salad made with tons of chopped hard-boiled eggs and sweet relish. For dessert, Mary Beth passes around brownies topped with ice cream made with— yummy—real vanilla. I know the vanilla is real because there are tiny brown specks mixed in the white. At last, I slump in the chair, totally stuffed.

"That was so good," I moan.

It's almost dark now; the sun's setting behind the house. Nana lights torches filled with oil that she says will keep mosquitoes away. It's like sitting in the middle of a giant birthday cake with all the candles lit. My perfect night would have included a couple of hours of video game playing, but this is a close second.

"Henry, can you please take our plates up to the house?" Nana asks. She can't fool me, I know this is code for it's time for adult conversation, and they don't want me to hear. Mom nods agreement at me, so I stack the plates and trudge back up the hill to the house. After I scrape and put them and the forks into the dishwasher, I find my iPod. At least I have music to listen to. I plug in the earphones, turn the volume down really low, and walk back down to where everyone is sitting. I take a chair and turn it around to face the ocean, so my back is to Mom, Nana, and my aunties. Then I pretend I'm listening to my music. Like I said, not an A student for nothing.

I don't know what they were talking about before, but I hear Mary Beth snuffling and then a noise as someone moves a chair. I turn around to look. Nana has her arm around Mary Beth and she's doing a pat, pat, on her back. Mom is using a stick to draw something in the sand between her feet. She looks over, sees me, and motions for me to turn around again.

Stinky jellyfish, caught.

I hit pause on the music, better to hear that way. Mary Beth is complaining. Something about Grandpa John not letting her go to the prom. Nana mutters something I can't hear.

"Good God," Rita says. She has a loud voice so there's no problem hearing her. "Way I remember it, you had crappy grades that year. That's why Dad said no. Quit feeling sorry for yourself. We all had it tough. Did I ever tell you about the time Dad got drunk and chased off my boyfriend by firing a shotgun? All because of an innocent kiss."

"You were never innocent," Mary Beth zings.

"Stop, both of you," my mom commands.

"Right, baby sister," Rita says. "You got to miss out on all the drunk drama. Guess you don't have anything to complain about. You always got everything you wanted, anyway."

"I didn't have any control over what went on before I was born. Besides, it was our mom who always got the brunt of it. Did you forget that? We always knew we could leave home after high school. She had to stay. Of course, Dad died shortly after we were grown and gone, but at least we could see an escape to the drinking and the angry, dry drunk problems. Mom here, she was stuck with him forever. And don't forget, she deflected a lot of Dad's meanness."

She goes on, "Mom, thank you for protecting us. I know you did the best that you could."

"You're right, I guess," Mary Beth sighs. "Thank you, Momma."

Rita grunts but doesn't say anything.

I hear shuffling and turn around to see them in a group hug. They have rearranged their chairs tighter into a circle and are talking low so I can't hear. When I glance around, they're even holding hands. Mushy time.

There are lights out in the ocean, and I cup my hands like binoculars to focus. Must be a ship. Something makes a big splash but whatever it was, it's gone too quickly to see.

"Mom," I whisper, going to where they're huddled. "Does Nana have any binoculars?"

Nana looks up. "They're in the drawer in the kitchen island, Henry. Go look if you want."

That's just where I find them. I sit on the edge of the deck, legs dangling through the railing posts, and watch until the ship with lights moves out of sight. Then I go back inside to read one of the books I brought. I hate not having television.

CHAPTER FOUR

THE NEXT DAY IS THE SAME: EXPLORE OUR PART OF THE island, swim with Mom, dinner on the beach, no television or Internet. The only things different are that Mom makes me stay away from the jungle and we have barbecued chicken and cornbread for supper. After dinner, the grownups do the same boring thing: talk, talk, hug, hug around the campfire.

Aunt Rita is talking on the phone when I come into the kitchen the third morning. The phone is weird. It's blue, big, and mounted on the wall. The part that Rita is talking into is linked to the wall phone by a curly blue cord. Jeeps, so very last century.

"Of course, I sent the material," Aunt Rita is saying in a loud voice. "The package is probably sitting on the idiot's desk somewhere. What? What? I can't hear you," Rita slaps the side of the phone, listens, says, "hello, hello," then bangs the phone back on the hook.

"This crappy phone has to be fifty years old," she says. "Who lives in the U.S. anymore without cell phones?" She glares at the wall phone. "Or at least a cordless phone. One that works!"

She stomps away.

"Mom said the phone service comes and goes," my

mom tells her. "Either the reception is bad, or the owner forgets to pay the bill."

"Is Mom supposed to pay it?" Rita asks.

My mom shrugs. "Don't know anything about that or the utilities."

Rita picks up the phone again, listens, then puts it back on the hook. "Good, a dial tone."

Mom, I see, is making pancakes. My stomach growls.

"Yummy. Are they done yet?"

"Almost," Mom answers and gives me a quick hug. "By the time you get the butter out of the fridge and your plate ready, they will be."

Mary Beth slouches out of her room. She has on a raggedy bathrobe. On her feet are these dumb "Hello Kitty" slippers. I look at my mom, widen my eyes, and when Mary Beth opens the fridge, I point to my auntie's feet. Mom puts a finger to her lips telling me to keep quiet, but I see she's smiling.

"Those sure smell good," Mary Beth says, scooting up onto the counter stool. "I'm starving. You, too, Henry?"

I start to say something but Rita interrupts. "Pancakes are the worst thing you can eat for breakfast, you know. All that sugary syrup and butter on top of those carbohydrates. Ugh."

"You don't have to eat 'em," my mom says.

Rita pulls a yogurt container out of the fridge and opens it.

"Those fruity yogurts have almost as much sugar as pancakes, you know," Mom adds, and shovels two cakes onto my plate.

"Me next," Mary Beth says and holds out her plate. "I guess since you're older you have to be more careful about what you eat, Sis. Me, I've always believed the day should start with a substantial breakfast. After all, you have all day to work the calories off."

"Twenty-three months isn't what I would call that much older," Rita snaps and hops up onto a counter stool on the other side of me.

"Mom's not up yet?" my mom asks them. "I know she likes flaps, but they're not good after they get cold."

Mom looks at me, expectantly. I know she's going to ask me to knock on Nana's door. I take a big bite, getting ready. Before Mom can ask me, Rita hops down from the stool and knocks softly on Nana Belle's door.

"Mom, Mom? You up yet? Jen's made us pancakes. Mom?"

There is no sound from Nana's room. Rita shrugs and comes back. "All our talking must have worn her out. We'll just let her sleep in."

"Last night at the beach, she said she planned to finish her wine and watch the moon for a while," my mom tells her. "Mary Beth, you were still up reading when I went to bed. Did you see her come back?"

"Nope. I just finished the chapter and went to my room. Rita?"

"I was out like a light. Didn't hear a damn anything."

"Maybe she fell asleep in the beach chair. They really are comfortable."

"I'll go check," Rita says. "The sun's up, and she's going to burn if she stays outside too long." She slips off her chair to check, but not before she tears a big chunk off of one of the pancakes that Mom has stacked on a plate.

I fork one more onto my plate but leave the one that Rita tore. I'm spreading butter across it when someone screams.

"Is that one of those damn gulls?" Mary Beth asks.

"No!" shouts Mom. She's already running toward the sliding door that opens onto the deck and beach.

My auntie and I follow. I'm much faster than Mary Beth so I get there quicker.

I stop where the chairs are all still lined up facing the sea. Rita has her hands over her mouth like she is trying to stop another scream. Mom is squatted by Nana's chair, and I see she is holding her wrist. The back of Nana Belle's head is leaning out a little from one side of the chair, the breeze making her puffy gray hair move. Except for her hair, Nana is still. This looks bad.

Everything is quiet, then my mom yells at Mary Beth who has finally huffed up. "I can't find a pulse."

"Move over," Mary Beth shouts, breathing hard. She rubs Nana's chest hard, making her head wobble, and says in a loud voice. "Momma, Momma, wake up."

She stops, turns to mom and Rita. "Put the back of the chair flat. I'll start CPR. Henry," she points at me, "run back to the house and call 911. Tell them we need the medics, Stat."

Mom adds, "Tell them where we are. You remember the name of this island, right?"

I turn and run as fast as I can back up the beach to the house saying the name of our island over and over, so I won't forget.

CHAPTER FIVE

"She looked so peaceful, just sitting there like she was watching the sun rise."

That's what Aunt Rita keeps saying as we wait in a room in the hospital for the doctor to come and talk to us. We've been in here a long time. There's no television or magazines so everyone just stares at the paintings hanging on the wall. I'm thinking that's why they call it a waiting room; all we've been doing is waiting.

I'm texting back and forth with Dad since we're back on the mainland with cell reception. He's on the way to the airport in a taxi. He asks how Mom and I are doing. I text back that we're okay and tell him about the helicopter landing on the sand.

Mary Beth had started CPR, but by the time I ran back to them, they had stopped and were covering Nana with a couple of striped towels. They moved their chairs away from where she was and were crying and talking quietly. I sat down beside Mom and pushed the dry sand into shapes. I've shot globs of aliens before in my games, but I'd never seen a real dead person. It's not the same, especially since it's my nana.

"It doesn't seem fair," my mom is saying now while

we wait for the doctor. "She had so much to look forward to. Now it's too late."

We're all quiet for a while.

Rita says, "I notified Stan Daniels back home. He's going to call the funeral home, the same one that handled Dad's funeral, and check on arrangements. He's also going to draft an obituary and send it to us so we can approve it and forward it to the local paper."

"Thanks for doing that," my mom says. She sniffs and wipes her nose. "I don't even know where to start." She looks at each of her sisters. "Did Mom ever talk to you about what she wants when, well, you know, I mean, her final arrangements?"

"Only thing I heard her say was that we should do what we thought best," Mary Beth says.

"Well, that doesn't help," snaps Rita. "She bought a headstone for Dad, but it's a small one, not a lot of space to add her name."

"Put her to rest beside Dad?" This is Mom talking.

"I don't know. Seems a little cruel that the poor woman has to spend eternity with a man who treated her so rudely in life," sighs Rita.

No one says anything. Dad texts that he's at the airport going through security. I show the message to Mom, and she nods.

"But it's always tradition that when the last spouse dies, they're buried beside each other." Mary Beth says.

"Not always," says Rita. Sometimes there's a family plot where everyone ends up. Sometimes the widow or widower remarries, and they are laid to rest beside the second spouse."

"How do we get Momma's body back to Nebraska, anyway. Isn't that expensive?" asks Mary Beth.

Everyone just looks at her. "Oh, I forgot for a minute. Guess that's not really an issue now."

There's a tap on the door and a doctor enters. She's holding an iPad.

"First I want to convey my condolences," the doctor says. "I'm Dr. Addelson, by the way. I was here when the air ambulance brought in your mom."

"Do you know what happened yet?" asks Rita.

"I suspect it was her heart. I talked to her primary care physician back in Nebraska. He told me she's been on medications for her heart for several years. We'll know more after the autopsy."

Mary Beth gasps. "Is that necessary?"

"Yes," the doctor says. "We have to do one for any unattended death."

She turns to me and explains, "That's a death where there was no medical personnel in attendance."

I nod at Dr. Addelson. I already knew that. Hello, educational television, although being Nana, it isn't the same as watching on TV.

"Our staff can do the autopsy tomorrow," the doctor continues. "We won't have the results for a few days, but we can release her body. You'll need to arrange for a pickup."

She stops talking and pinches her lips together until they almost disappear. She doesn't look very doctorly when she does that.

Then she says, "What I mean is, you'll need to make arrangements with a local funeral home. They'll work with the one in Mrs. McNally's hometown for transport of her body back for services and burial. Are there any other next of kin besides you three?"

"No," Rita says.

"What about Stephen and my girls," chimes in Mary Beth.

"The doctor means immediate next-of-kin, not the grandkids and in-laws," declares Rita.

"That doesn't mean they're not kin," says Mary Beth in the whiny voice.

The doctor stares at Mary Beth and then at Rita. Mom is focused on the picture hanging on the wall beside Dr. Addelson.

"Okay then," says the doctor as she stands up fast. "I'll just get the paperwork started, and you can figure out the logistics. Just let us know when you've decided on the funeral home."

We go to a different waiting room and do what? Snap, we wait and wait some more. At least this one has windows. There's a lady at a desk answering the phone. Every time she hangs up it starts ringing again. Dad is on the plane so I can't text him. Mom calls funeral homes, then she calls motels. Mary Beth goes downstairs to the cafeteria and brings us back sandwiches and sodas.

"Stan Daniels is going to fly out and meet us here," Rita says folding her phone. She does not look happy. "Says he's going to bring along Mom's will and the trust documents."

Rita's face gets tight, and her lips disappear like the doctor's had. Her phone doinks, saying a text came in. She looks at it and frowns.

"Well?" Mom asks Rita. "What did he say? You were on the phone with him for a long time."

"Stan Daniels has way outlived his ability to work with the law. Apparently, Mom did have him draw up the trust documents, but she wanted to wait to draft a new will until after she returned."

"That was his idea?" Mom asks.

"No, our mother's idea. She wanted to have this family reunion with us first. If the old coot had been competent, he would have convinced Mom to redo her will at the same time."

"You think she planned to cut some of us out of the will?" Mary Beth's voice sounds uncertain.

"I don't know what she had planned." She waves her hand toward the receptionist sitting behind the desk. "It's not like we can ask Mom now. Anyway, Daniels is on his way here. He'll read the old will to us and then we can figure out what to do next."

"He tell you who's going to inherit?" Mary Beth asks, again in the uncertain voice.

"Nope, wants to meet with us first."

Mary Beth looks at Aunt Rita and then at Mom. "You know, Stephen and I were always the ones who watched out for Momma since you both lived so far away. I'm not saying we minded, hear me, even if the drive from Omaha to Mom took a couple of hours. I'm just saying that we helped the most."

Both Rita and my mom give my aunt a hard look.

Rita says, "Are you saying that you deserve more? I'm the one who always paid the taxes and insurance on her house."

"I didn't say anything like that."

"You're saying Stephen helped Mom out?" my mom asks. "Doing what? You heard her; the house was falling apart. She doesn't even like him. Mom told me he was the laziest realtor she'd ever seen. Said Stephen told her before she even won the money that he wanted to sell her house so she could move into a little condo. Told her that way she could help out the grandkids more. And, of course, he'd take his usual commission."

"Stephen never."

"He did."

Other people in the waiting room had turned around to watch us. I tap Mom's arm. "Inside voice," I whisper.

All three of them stop talking, but they're still glaring at each other.

Quietly, Rita says, "Let's just wait until Stan reads the will. We were her only family." Then in a lower voice, she adds, "and remember this was written before the L-O-T-T-E- R-Y".

Like everyone in the waiting room can't spell lottery.

She goes on. "I know Mom loved us all. It's not like she even had enough money back then to will it to Adopt-a-Dog or some charity like that instead of us. If I was to guess, I'd say equal shares to each of us."

"What about the house?" Mary Beth asks.

Rita snorts. "Well, if you want to buy it from the estate with your inheritance, you just go ahead. I don't want it."

"Me neither," Mom agrees.

"I don't want to live in it either," Mary Beth says. "It's just that Stephen would like the listing."

Rita rolls her eyes and we're all quiet for a while.

Then Rita adds, "The one thing that I did learn from Daniels is that Mom told him she wanted to be cremated."

Mary Beth shudders.

"Then do what with the ashes?" my mom asks.

"Hell if I know. There might be instructions in the will. If not, we can decide. But let's not worry about that yet. Right now, we need to find a local funeral home to pick her up."

CHAPTER SIX

THE NEXT MORNING, WE'RE SITTING AROUND A TABLE IN a corner of the motel's big room; a conference room, Mom had explained earlier. Rita was right, Mr. Daniels is old. His hair is mostly gone and there are big freckle things on his head and arms. On the table is a funny-looking, scratched leather case with straps and buckles that he's so slowly undoing. I see Rita glance at my mom and give a little shake of her head.

"No talking, no fidgeting, and no playing games on your Nintendo," she had told me before we rode the elevator down from our room to here. So boring. I yawn, and my mom motions for me to cover my mouth.

Old Mr. Daniels finally gets the case open and arranges files and papers on the table. Mary Beth is closest to him, and she tilts her head and squints, trying to read them. I don't think she can since her reading glasses are on top of her head.

He clears his throat. Loudly. Rita jumps.

"As I said before, I am very sorry to hear of Belle's death. My condolences to you all. I've known, knew her, for a long time. Knew your dad, too. Handled his probate, seems like just yesterday. Anyway, it's too bad that Belle didn't have much of a chance to enjoy her winnings. Did I ever tell you about how I first met your mom and dad?"

Rita gives him the squint eye. Dad likes to watch old cowboy movies where the good guy does that same thing. My aunt would make a good gunslinger.

"Never mind," Mr. Daniels says. "I know you young folks, especially you, young man," he looks at me, "have more important things to do than to hear me ramble on."

Mom pinches the skin between her eyes. Mary Beth looks at the ceiling and mumbles something.

"Let me start with the trust document," he says and passes out a file to each of my aunts and my mom. "You'll find it's pretty straightforward. Belle was the trustee of the Belle McNally Family Trust. Before she passed, she had the discretion to use, sell, or dispose of the trust assets in any manner she wished. I assisted her in retitling the assets and setting up the majority of her financial accounts in the name of the trust. That includes her house. It excludes her 1997 Pontiac; that remains solely in her name.

"The biggest assets in the trust are two brokerage accounts. One account is invested long-term in stocks and bonds, mostly blue-chip companies. The other account holds financial instruments that provide an income for her and more liquid assets that she can use as she wishes, wished, I mean. There's also money in a bank checking and bank savings account. She set up educational savings accounts for the grandkids, and annual deposits have already been established so money automatically flows to them from the second brokerage account."

Mom nods at this.

He pauses, looks at each of us. "The trust says that after Belle, the trustee, dies a successor trustee will be appointed."

Rita starts to speak but he interrupts. "Your mom wanted to be fair, so she selected all three of you to serve as trustees." He shook his head. "I tried to explain that appointing multiple trustees can sometimes be a nightmare if they don't agree, but Belle was adamant that she wanted all three of you to work together. You three are the beneficiaries of the trust, as well as the joint trustees after her death. As I said, the accounts have already been set up and the assets transferred to the trust. That was the hardest part. The rest is up to you three."

Mary Beth asks, "You said money is in easy-to-access accounts?"

"As I said, one of the brokerage accounts is set up in long-term, illiquid investments. The other brokerage account and the bank accounts are more liquid."

"How much?" Mary Beth asks again.

"There's around fifteen million in the long-term account. More than that in the second investment account. A good portion of those funds, I want to warn you, will need to be used to pay her income and estate taxes. She has ...had an accountant, and he has already calculated what will be needed to pay her income and other taxes this year. There's several million in bank savings accounts. Belle had planned to disburse the majority of that to you girls."

"How much?" Rita asks.

"She didn't say. I recommended that she disburse the funds over several years to avoid gift taxes or set up a trust for that purpose, but she didn't tell me the specifics of what she was planning.

"Of course, things have changed now with her death. I suggest you hire a good accountant. There's a little over two hundred thousand in her checking account. That is readily available to pay her last expenses and funeral arrangements."

"We can use one of the accountants in our firm," Rita suggests.

"Just a minute," Mom says. "We're working as a team on this, remember."

"A team," echoes Mary Beth.

Rita says, "I'm just saying that I have contacts through my firm that can help."

"I think someone independent would be better," Mom says.

"There's a bunch of accountants in Omaha where we live," says Mary Beth.

"And you have a feeling who's more competent, I suppose," Rita says.

"Haven't you heard of the Yellow Pages? I'm sure we can find someone closer."

"Closer to you?" Mom snaps.

Mr. Daniels taps a spoon against his coffee cup.

"Ladies, let's not argue. I'm sure we can figure out something that works for everyone."

This is going to be interesting to watch, I think, but not in a good way.

"Sure," cracks Rita. "Now, about Mom's will."

He slowly bends down and pulls another file folder out of his case. He opens it and looks at them for a long time: first at Rita, at Mary Beth, then at Mom. He does not look happy.

"Like I mentioned on the phone, this is an old will. Before Belle won the lottery, the estate was simple, and the will reflects that."

"Just get on with it," Rita snaps. She's tapping her foot under the table.

"She loved all three of you, understand," he says.

"Ah, crap," Rita says. "What did she do?"

"No really, she loved all three of you the same. It's just that...," he pauses. "Your mom wasn't naive, and her mind was as sharp as it was when she wrote this will. It was written, however, about fifteen years ago. Not long after your dad died."

Tap, tap goes my aunt's foot.

"Her biggest regret was that the three of you never did get along."

Tap, tap.

"So, back when the estate wasn't worth much, this wasn't a big deal. Now, it may be."

"Oh, Jesus," Mary Beth moans. "Don't tell me she left everything to some charity or her church. Hell, she hardly went to church. Just Easter and Christmas when my family went with her."

"No, not the church," he says.

"The Humane Society?" my mom asks.

There are going to be a lot of happy dogs and cats. Mom will for sure let me have a puppy now.

"No."

"Then what?" all three say in unison.

"Belle's intent with the will, and that includes what's in the trust, was that it be divided between the three of you."

Mom and Aunt Mary Beth relax. Rita still looks tense.

"But?" Rita says. "I hear a 'but' after that."

Mr. Daniels clears his throat. "The will says that the three of you have to reside together, that is stay together, for a month, thirty days actually, in her home. If any of you quit the residence before that month is out, then that daughter forfeits her share."

"That is the most ridiculous provision I ever heard of," declares Rita.

"But school starts in three weeks," adds my mom.

"I can't be stuck there, away from Omaha, all by myself, that long," whines Mary Beth.

"Nana's house is so boring," I whisper to Mom. "There's nothing to do in Nebraska."

"As I said, Mrs. McNally desired that you all get along. It wasn't a big deal when it was just the house and an old vehicle, and whatever personal property she owned. If one of you wanted to leave before the thirty days were up, then it was not a big loss. Now, of course, her net worth is a lot bigger."

He looks at everyone again and shakes his head.

They were already fighting. I know this is just going to be worse.

I tap on Mom's arm to get her attention. "Can I just stay with Dad?"

"We'll see," Mom whispers.

Everyone's quiet while they read their copy of the will. I lean across Mom and try to read, but it doesn't make much sense.

"Mom," I whisper. "Can I have some money for a soda?"

"Sure, sure." She digs into her purse.

"Some chips, too?"

"Yes, here. Come right back, okay?"

She hands me four dollars. Nice. Enough for a soda, chips, and maybe a Snickers.

"Ridiculous," Rita is saying when I come back. She's the first one done reading.

Mary Beth points to something on the page and asks Mr. Daniels what it means.

"Couldn't you have talked her out of this?" Rita asks Mr. Daniels. "I've been an attorney for years and I've never seen anything as convoluted."

"This is what your mom wanted. I advised her to do something different, but it was her choice to make. You should know that I have to write what a client wants."

"Isn't there something we can do? Challenge it?" my mom says.

"As you see," he says, "there's a clause at the end that says if the will is challenged, then that heir will be disinherited. That means if one of you protests any terms of the will, then you don't inherit."

"Unless the will is fraudulent, or Mom didn't have the mental capacity to sign," Rita says.

Mr. Daniels frowns at Rita. He doesn't look so old or creaky when he does that.

Rita throws up her hands. "Okay, okay. I guess Mom wasn't any more demented when she signed it than she was last night or the night before."

"Momma certainly wasn't crazy." Mary Beth crosses her arms across her front and glares at her sister.

Everyone is quiet for a while. Rita is reading the will again. Mary Beth excuses herself to go to the bathroom. Mom's texting Dad, who had stayed in our room to work on the computer. Mr. Daniels is putting stuff back into his case. He looks like he can't wait to leave. Me, too.

Rita taps her fingers on the table and says to Mr. Daniels, "The will says that we have to stay at Mom's home. But what if she has established residency somewhere else? Couldn't we just stay at the beach house? At least it's not Boonieville, Nebraska."

"I'd say that if Belle has legally established residency somewhere else, then that's considered her home at the time of her death. How long did she plan on staying on the island?"

"She rented it through October and was having her mail delivered to the post office in town. The ferry brings it out to her. She's paying the utilities there during the lease period. To me, she planned to live there until at least October. To me, all of that means Mom has established residency."

"Plus, she mentioned that she was thinking of selling the old house and buying a condo on the beach," adds my mom.

"What's going on?" asks Mary Beth, wading into the room.

They explain. Mr. Daniels nods his head. "That might work. Long as the three of you agree."

Everyone nods. Including me. If I can talk Mom into getting a television, and satellite Internet, I'd be set. Plus, I could find out what's on the other side of the jungle since Mom interrupted me before.

"If you are all in agreement, it should be okay. Staying at Belle's temporary residence doesn't go against either what's expressly written in the will or your mother's intent, so I don't see any issue with it."

He pauses, thinking. "I'll warn you that all three of you need to be firm on agreeing to stay at her leased house. If just one of you dissents, then it will be up to the courts to determine."

Rita gives long looks at both of her sisters. "Are we all in agreement that the three of us McNally girls will spend our month at Mom's beach house?" Rita asks.

"Yes," everyone agrees.

"We can buy a television and get Internet service?" I ask.

"Well," Mr. Daniels says, drawing out the word.

This does not sound good.

"If we're going to look at Belle's intent, then I suggest that you do nothing against what she set out to do."

"I'm going back home with Dad then," I whisper to Mom.

Everyone looks at Mr. Daniels.

"Belle's will requires you three daughters to reside together for thirty days. She told me before she left that she chose that island because there were no distractions like television and such. Did she say anything like that to you?"

Mom shrugs. Rita frowns. Mary Beth says, "I may recall her saying something like that."

Spider toenails. No Internet. No television. Going back home with Dad sounds better and better.

"What about Henry?" Mary Beth asks.

"There's nothing in that provision of the will that addresses spouses or children."

"We'll talk to your dad," Mom says, patting my leg.

"Now," Mr. Daniels says, "Let's talk about funeral arrangements."

They talk, I play my game, half listening. Nana's going to get cremated at the funeral home. Mr. Daniels says he already emailed the obituary they saw last night to the newspaper in Nana's town in Nebraska. A memorial service will be held later, after the month in the beach house.

"So, send Mom's ashes back home?" asks my mom.

"What did Momma say about what to do with her ashes?" asks Mary Beth.

"Nothing," the lawyer says. "You'll have to decide. They can be interred, scattered somewhere, or kept in an urn."

"Buried with Dad," suggests Mary Beth.

"We could scatter them here in South Carolina, on the beach or in the sea," says mom.

"That's just not right."

"Either of you want to keep the urn with her ashes?" asks Rita.

Mary Beth shudders.

Mom says, "Not really. I prefer to remember her the way she was."

"You could have them placed in a nice urn and then decide over the month what you want to do with them," Mr. Daniels interjects.

"You mean like keep them in the beach house?" asks Mary Beth.

"Sure. It won't hurt to keep them there. It reinforces the residency clause," Rita says.

"That's creepy," I tell Mom on the elevator back to our room. "Dead Nana Belle in a jar?"

"Just her ashes," explains Mom, frowning. "You remember how your Grandma Grace keeps Puddles' little silver urn of ashes on the mantle of her fireplace? It's like that. Just a little metal container that we'll put somewhere. It'll be like Nana Belle's watching over us."

Mom seems mad so I don't say anything else, just think about Nana Belle in a silver urn. I guess it wouldn't be much different than Grandma Grace's dead dog. Except, I never knew Puddles. He died before I was born. Nana Belle, I know.

Mom stomps into the room when we get back from talking with Mr. Daniels, goes into the bathroom, and slams the door. Dad says, "Uh oh." After Mom comes out, they go out onto the balcony and slide the glass door shut behind them.

I turn on the TV, find Cartoon Network, and watch it and Mom and Dad at the same time. SpongeBob waves his hands. Mom waves her hands and talks a lot. Dad listens. Then Mom cries and Dad hugs her. SpongeBob talks to Patrick, but they don't hug. The show ends. When they come inside Mom goes straight to the bathroom, again. She's still crying a little and sniffing a lot.

"Hey, buddy," Dad says to me. "How about we go out somewhere for lunch, just the two of us."

I'm happy to leave.

"Can we eat at Wendy's?" I ask. It's my favorite place to eat but not Dad's.

"Sure, kid," he says with no trying to convince me that Burger King is better. Strange, but then everything seems strange lately.

"Is Mom going to be okay?" I ask after we pick up our tray and find a place to sit.

"She'll be okay, Henry. She's sad about Nana dying.

Life's been a roller coaster lately, you know that, and this has been hard. First, she was happy that your nana won the money and that she could spend some beach time with her. Then Nana dies, and now she learns she's stuck there for a month with your aunties. She's just trying to find her footing."

"I'm sad, too," I say. "Nana wants to get burned up. Why?"

"Cremated. Some people want to be buried in a coffin like your Grandpa John. You weren't even born when he died. Other people want to be cremated. Think of it like traveling to heaven and touching the sun. You know, like how good the sun feels when you're cold."

Dad stops talking. He puts a hand on my shoulder and rubs it. For some reason, it makes me want to burrow under his arm and cry like when I was a little kid. I blink, blink again. I am so not going to cry at Wendy's.

"Did your mom explain what happens when a person is cremated?"

"Not really," I tell him.

"Sometimes, I forget how much you've grown. Not a baby anymore, you."

Hello, almost eleven.

"When a body is cremated, they're put in a very hot kiln. The flames break down the body until there's nothing but ashes."

"It doesn't hurt?"

"No, son. The part that was your nana—her personality, her soul, the things that made her who she was inside—that part of her is already in heaven. The only thing left is the physical body, and it no longer feels pain after we die. It's like when we eat corn. Think of the husk as Nana's body and the corn as her soul. The husk contains the soul, the corn. When we're ready to eat the corn, we don't need the husks anymore. Does that make it easier to understand?"

"What about the cob after we eat the corn?"

Dad laughs. I love to hear him laugh.

"I guess that wasn't the best example."

"Nana's body after she died is like the husk or the cob," I say.

"Yes."

"And we can just throw it into the fire like when we go camping."

"Sort of like that."

"And what about Nana's ashes? What are we supposed to do with them?"

"That would be up to your mom and aunties."

I take the last fry, dunk it in the ketchup, and chew.

"Do you think they'll just put Nana in a jar and put her on the bookshelf like Grandma Grace did with Puddles?"

"It's possible, but I seriously doubt your mom would want Nana's urn hanging out at our house. They may decide to bury the urn next to Grandpa John or scatter her ashes somewhere, the ocean maybe."

I shudder. I love Nana, but I didn't want to think about swimming and bumping into bits of her.

We crumple up the wrappers and take them to the trash. I take the cup with me since I didn't drink all my soda.

We walk down the sidewalk toward the motel and Mom.

"Dad," I say when we get closer to the motel, "Mom, Aunt Mary Beth, and Aunt Rita argue a lot. Why?"

"It's not that your mom dislikes her sisters. It's just that the three of them live very different lives. And they all have opinions." He smiles. "They're good at expressing those opinions, too."

Like, I so know that.

"Are you enjoying your time at the beach house?" Dad asks.

"It's okay, I guess. But there is no Internet and no television." I say the last very slowly so Dad can see the seriousness.

He laughs.

Snap, did he think this wasn't a problem?

"Like the Dark Ages," he says, still laughing.

"Like before fire was invented." I do not laugh.

"Like before fish walked onto land?"

"Like that," I agree.

He gets a serious look. "You could come back with me, but I'm still up to my ears in the project. You'd have to spend days with Grandma Grace. She does have a television."

"Yes, but we both have to watch the same channel and she likes old people stuff."

"As in?"

"Jeopardy. And the ones she watches in the afternoon, her stories, she calls them."

"Pond scum," Dad says.

"Squirmy stuff living in pond scum," I say.

We see an ice cream store and go in. After we eat the cones, Dad buys some more to take back to Mom.

"So, son, you'll have to decide. Is it Grandma Grace and Jeopardy or Mom and the beach house?" asks Dad as we start back.

I tell him about the island and the beach and what I had glimpsed of the house through the jungle. I tell him I climbed a tree but not how high.

"Cool," he says.

"There is more fun stuff to do at Nana Belle's, I guess. Plus, Grandma Grace's Internet connection is sooo slooow."

Mom seems happier when we get back.

"You brought me ice cream?" she says when she sees the sack. "My two favorite guys."

"We're your only guys," Dad and I say in unison. It's a family joke thing.

Mom kisses me on my cheek and Dad on the lips then pulls the container out of the sack.

"Rita, Bethie, and I went for lunch and decided on a plan for staying at the beach house," she tells us. "We're making a grocery and supplies list, and we can buy enough provisions now to last us for the time we're there. The store will put the order together and ferry half of it out. Then in two weeks, they'll send out the rest of the order by ferry. If we need anything else, we raise the flag at the dock, the ferry captain takes our order, and then brings it to us in a day or so."

"Complicated, but seems like it will work," Dad says. "When is all this going to start?"

Mom takes a big breath. She squishes her lips together. For a second, she looks just like Aunt Rita when she did that lip squishy thing.

"We're meeting at four o'clock today at the funeral home. They're handling the cremation; that will be done tonight. We're going to pick out an urn and settle the bill. Tomorrow, we'll purchase the food and supplies and arrange for delivery. Then the day after tomorrow, we pick up Mom's urn." She wipes her nose. "There's no reason to stay here after we have the ashes and supplies, so we'll leave for the island then."

"What did you two decide?" she asks us.

"I'm going to stay with you," I say.

Dad holds out cupped hands like they were sides of a scale. He lifts one. "Grandma Grace with two televisions, one channel that she selects, and very slow Internet service." He lifts the other hand. "The island, no Internet or TV, but lots of sand and adventure." He moves his hands up and down. "And the beach house wins."

Mom hugs me. "I'm glad you're going to be there with me."

"You think a DS and some new games breaks the no television or Internet rule?" I ask.

"Well, young man, I don't recall any specific prohibition mentioned, do you?"

I shake my head. Sweet.

Everyone rushes around the next few days: shopping for my gaming stuff, watching my aunties and mom write bunches of lists, driving Dad back to the airport, and returning the rental car. Mom only lets me buy two new games. I tell her that she's a millionaire now and what are a couple more games, but she says she doesn't want me to become spoiled. Chicken fart. Dad promises to send me another one when he gets back home.

I'm going to have a birthday while we're at Nana's beach house. Dad said turning eleven is a big deal so he's coming back for that. I'm glad because I'm going to miss him. Mom cannot, even with years of practice, pitch a good baseball. Now that I'm almost eleven, I bet I can hit a ball so far out into the ocean that even sharks can't find it.

Finally, we board the ferry: Mom, me, Rita, Mary Beth, tons of shopping bags and suitcases, and one urn-size cardboard box wrapped with packing tape, Nana Belle. I try not to think about that last thing.

CHAPTER SEVEN

I HAVE FUN THE FIRST FEW DAYS, SWIMMING WITH MOM and playing my new games. Today, Mom is busy doing her stuff and not watching me close, so I explore the forest. I'm still wondering what I saw past the trees on the other side of the island. That is until the ferry blows its horn announcing it's headed toward our dock, and I have to duck out of the trees before Mom sees me.

"Stay out of that jungle," she had ordered so I knew there would be trouble if she caught me in there.

"I thought for sure we got everything," Mom says as we start toward where the ferry is bumping up against the old tires hanging off the side of the dock.

"I bet it's the girls," adds Mary Beth. She's breathing hard as she passes us, going faster than I had ever seen her walk.

"What?" Rita says. "What did you say?" she asks again in case we didn't get it the first time.

"Oh, crap," says my mom, all quiet-like but I still hear it.

The ferryman is sliding out the ramp but I'm not watching that. Nose boogers, my cousins. Slimy, green nose boogers.

Heather is first down the ramp. She has on her

swimsuit top, and the first thing I notice is that her boobies are bigger than they were that Christmas at Nana Belle's old house.

Mom bumps my shoulder. "Don't stare, Henry."

Hard not to since she aimed those things at me, I want to say but don't.

"Hey, cousin," she says and smirks. The smirk is the same.

Mom bumps my shoulder again.

"Hey, Heather," I say, feeling all the fun leak out of the day.

I'm pulling on Mom's arm so she'll lean down, and I can ask why they're here when Mary Beth answers my question.

"You brought Henry so why can't I bring my family?"

"Stephen, too?" asks Rita. Her hands are on her hips, and she looks mad.

Just then Uncle Stephen comes through the ferry's doorway. He's handing something to the captain.

"Like I said," he tells the man, "here's my card. Look me up if your cousin is interested in buying that house. I'll hook her up with a real good price."

"Jesus Christ," Rita hisses to Mary Beth. "Don't tell me he's already trying to sell Mom's old house?"

Mary Beth acts like she doesn't hear. She hugs Heather, Sarah Beth, and Riley Rose. She tries to hug Stephen but he's picking up his bag and ignores her.

Besides the boobs, Heather has a big nose. She might be pretty except for the nose, and the smirky way she talks to everyone.

Sarah Beth looks a lot like her mom: chubby and slouchy. She and Heather always gang up on me, but it's mostly Heather's idea.

Riley Rose was just a baby the last time I saw her, crawling after her sisters on fat, baby legs. Now she's bigger with light brown curls that don't look anything like Heather's flat hair. She looks like one of my mom's old Kewpie dolls that she has stored in the closet, the one with the smile dimples.

Rita still looks mad.

"If I'd known you'd invite them," Rita pointed at Stephen and my cousins picking up their suitcases, "I'd have brought my friend, Jeffrey. Hell, I would have invited the whole office."

"Oh, Jeffrey," says Stephen, sounding out all the consonants in the name. "He's your latest beau, I suppose. What happened to what's his face that you brought with you when you came out at Christmas to visit Mom? Lance or Lawrence, whatever."

"Lowell, and what business is it of yours?"

"Nada," says Stephen. "Just seems like you go through them pretty fast."

"That's enough," my mom tells Stephen. "Henry, help your cousins grab their bags and we'll go back to the house."

Heather swings a bright pink bag at me, dangling from a strap around her wrist. "Here, carry this," she commands.

I ignore her. "Riley Rose, you want some help?" I grab her roller bag with Hello Kitty on it. My aunt and uncle have already started up the hill to the house. Stephen is in the lead, saying something, and making big gestures with his hands. Mary Beth is trudging behind with my uncle's biggest suitcase. Heather and Sarah Beth follow.

Riley Rose is slow, so everyone is already in the house when we get there. First thing I see is Heather moving all my stuff out of my bedroom.

"Hey, that's my room."

"Not anymore, Cuz. You're sharing a room with your mommy. This one belongs to me."

"Me, too," says Sarah Beth. "We're sharing."

"No, it's mine. I had it first."

"You'll have to bunk with me," my mom says. I see the worry wrinkle between her eyebrows. "We're short on rooms. Aunt Mary Beth and Stephen are going to use Nana Belle's old room. It's the biggest. You and I are in my room, there are two beds and plenty of space. Rita keeps her old room in the back. Riley Rose gets the small bedroom next to her mom and dad."

"It's not—," I start to say, but Mom puts a hand on my shoulder and whispers to me.

"I know, I know, but we'll just have to make do. It's only for a few weeks."

A very long few weeks. Frog squirt.

I carry my stuff to Mom's room. I start to leave, reconsider, and go back to tuck my new game player into my suitcase and shove it under the bed. I know how Heather thinks, and I'm not taking chances.

"Mom, I'm going outside," I tell her.

I've almost escaped when Heather says something that makes me a little happier.

"Mom," she says, using the grumpy voice. "I tried to text Sierra, but I can't get any service."

"No cell service here," I say, trying not to grin. "No Internet either. You should go back home."

Snap, Team Rowley hits one out of the park.

After I move my stuff into Mom's room, I sit on the couch and play Super Mario on my DS. It's one of my old games that Dad brought with him, and I've played it tons of times. That means it's a good game for spying since I know what's going to happen next and I can concentrate on what's being said in the kitchen. There, I don't know what's coming next.

Heather, Sarah Beth, and Riley are outside, lying on the deck in their swimsuits. Not very smart since the deck is in the shade and they can't tan. Uncle Stephen is somewhere with the fishing stuff he found.

Mom and my aunties had made a list of who is responsible for cooking dinner. Tonight, it's supposed to be Rita's turn to cook, but Mary Beth offered instead. I think she's trying to make nicey-nice since my uncle and the brats are here. I ate Rita's cooking before, so I know this is a good thing. Mom's helping Mary Beth. Rita is sitting at the kitchen bar with a glass of wine. It's not her first.

"I'm just saying that we still can make this work, you know," Rita is saying. "Thirty days, twenty-six now, and then life goes back to normal, and we inherit enough to make all our lives very comfortable." She takes a big drink of the wine and then holds out three fingers. "Thirty days, we can make this work, right?"

"Of course, we can," Mom says. "It's what our mom wanted."

Stephen comes back. His shorts are wet, and his flip-flops make squishing noises as he walks to the kitchen.

"Hell of a fish I almost caught," he tells everyone in a loud voice. "The son-of-a-bitch was two feet long, at least. Damn, if it didn't try to pull me in, and I had to cut my line. Should have brought the heavier line."

"Watch the language," my mom says and nods toward me. I play the game pretending I don't hear. Zoom goes Mario.

"Jeez, Jenny, the boy's what, almost eleven now? I'm sure he's heard swearing before. What's the problem, huh?"

"I'm telling you, we don't use that language at home, and I'm not going to listen to it here. There are five million words in the English language. I'm sure you can find others to use."

"Says the English major," Stephen says in a singsong

voice. "Hell, you never minded me speaking my mind, right, Mary Beth?"

"Well, I…" my aunt begins but Stephen interrupts.

"Screw, son-of-a-bitch, you know they're all words in the dictionary. That makes it official. Don't see why we can't say them. How about fornication, flatulence, vomit? They bad words, too?"

"That's enough," Rita snaps.

Mary Beth doesn't say anything.

"That's enough, that's enough," Stephen says in the singsong voice again. "Figures, surrounded by all this estrogen. Hey, Henry, you wanna go fishing with me? Get outta here and do some guy stuff."

"Maybe tomorrow," I mumble.

Stephen shrugs and goes squishing off to Nana Belle's old room. Before he gets there, he turns around and says, "That boy needs to quit playing that damn game and go outside or he's gonna turn into a sissy."

Mom stands up and says, "You better watch your mouth," but Uncle Stephen slams the bedroom door before she can get it all the way out.

I look at Mom. Her face is all red and she's glaring at Mary Beth who has her back turned trying to act busy.

Rita stomps over and marks a big red "X" over day four of the calendar she bought before we returned here. I want to say something about the day not being over yet, but Mario needs my help.

Mom and I eat at a table on the deck away from everyone else. There's fried chicken, kind of mushy but delicious; instant potatoes that Mary Beth stuck a whole stick of butter into the middle; cream gravy and biscuits with more butter and honey. Very yummy, but Mom's just playing with her food.

"Not a vegetable in sight," she mumbles, rubbing her forehead.

"There's cream corn," I say around a chunk of chicken. I like corn on the cob, but cream corn is too goopy, so I didn't get any.

"Mind if I join you two?" Rita asks, sliding the door open.

Mom waves her hand at the empty chair.

I'm not supposed to talk with my mouth full, so I don't say anything.

"What did she do to this chicken?" Mom asks. "It's soft and bland."

"Said she steamed it after it was fried," says Rita. She shrugs. "Not that I know much about cooking. There are so many great restaurants in Chicago. Who needs a stove?"

"I'm surprised you can stay so thin eating out all the time," Mom says.

"To-go boxes," Rita explains. "One meal out will last me several days. Now that one," she points a fork at me. "I bet he never needs a doggy bag."

I lean back and pat my belly.

"Mom, can I have—" I start to say but she interrupts.

"You've had enough, young man."

I watch Rita scrape the crust off her chicken. The only other thing on her plate is a naked biscuit, no butter or honey. She cuts the meat into little cubes and chews each one very slowly.

"No vegetables and all this starch," my mom says to Rita. "Not very healthy."

Just then Mary Beth opens the patio door and leans out, "There's more if anyone's hungry."

"No thanks," Mom and Rita say at the same time.

"I'm good," I say, catching Mom's look.

"Explains a lot," my mom mumbles as Mary Beth closes the door.

We're all quiet for a while. Rita puts another

chicken cube in her mouth and chews while looking out at the ocean.

"My turn tomorrow," Rita says. "I'll have Stephen grill steaks."

I ask Mom to excuse me, and I take my plate in and put it in the sink.

"You're doing dishes," Sarah Beth snarks.

"Not," I say. Hello, there's a dishwasher.

I make sure my DS is hidden in the bedroom before I go back outside.

CHAPTER EIGHT

It rains in the night, but by morning all the clouds have gone. I could have slept later but a loud noise wakes me up. Stephen is running the blender in the kitchen Mom and I discover when we go see what the buzzing is all about.

"My health drink," he tells us, patting his tummy. "Have it every morning. Detoxes my whole body. That and an early run on the beach."

He adds ice cubes, turns on the blender. *Whir, whine, crunch, crunch.*

Rita opens her bedroom door and throws a pillow at him. "Shut that damn thing off, will you. How do you expect us to get any sleep around here with that noise, huh?" She slams her door shut.

Stephen ignores her. Mom has her hands over her ears.

The blender stops. "Try it," he says, pouring some into a cup and pushing it toward Mom. "It has whey powder, apple juice, banana, and dried greens. There's powdered green tea added for wake-up power."

"Pass," Mom says and goes back to our room.

"Me, too."

I open the fridge and take out a milk carton.

Mom and I are going swimming this morning. I have on my swim trunks but no shirt. My uncle pokes my arm.

"No muscle tone there, kid. You need to get on a regimen like me. I do push-ups and sit-ups every morning, run a couple of miles and then drink a high-protein breakfast. Now I'm like this." He has on a muscle shirt, and he holds up an arm and flexes the muscle. I turn back to the fridge so he can't see my big grin. Even Spider-Man has bigger muscles than that.

"See what I mean?" my uncle says. "Of course, your dad probably doesn't set a good example, him being one of those computer nerds."

"My dad plays baseball with me all the time," I tell him. "And he's very strong," I add just in case he didn't get it. I pour milk into a glass, squirt in some Hershey's chocolate, and stir.

"Right," he says, drawing it out to make it sound not right at all.

Mom swims and I use the boogie board I found in the plastic storage box under the deck. I wade in and hop on the board when the water gets to my waist. I'm wearing the life vest mom made me wear and it squeaks when I lie on my stomach and slide to the front. I paddle out, and when I see a big wave coming, I turn to face the beach and try to stand. *Splash*, a wave jerks the board away and I'm down. I swallow salty water and choke, but I keep hold of the board.

I try again and again until finally I can almost stand up before, *plunk*, I'm in the water again. Surfing is harder than it looks.

Mom is swimming back and forth, along the beach, between the sand and me. I catch a wave, stand, fall off, *splash*. After the millionth time, I do it. Wobbly, but I'm up and moving. Victory.

After a while, I see Mom walk toward the beach

chair and her towel. *Splash*, and I'm swallowing salty water again. Enough.

"Why did Uncle Stephen and the brats have to come and spoil everything?" I ask Mom when I join her. We've spread our towels on the beach and we're on our stomachs, backs to the sun and ocean. "I thought Nana Belle just wanted you and my aunties here."

Mom's been reading a book. She puts in the book-mark to hold her place, closes it, and rubs her forehead.

"That was the plan but, of course, everything's changed now that your nana's gone," she says.

"I know, but...," I say.

She sits up, rummages in her bag, and pulls out the sunscreen. She squirts lotion on her hands and rubs it on her shoulders and the back of her neck. Finally, she talks.

"Not much I can say now. I brought you so I can't really argue about Mary Beth wanting her family here, too."

"But I was here before. Nana said it was okay I came. And Dad's not here."

Now Mom's spreading sunscreen on my back. I try to squirm away. I hate the feel of it—greasy gunky.

"Be still, Henry. I don't want you to get burned."

"Mom, Uncle Stephen said Dad's a computer nerd. He's so dumb."

She laughs. I love Mom's laugh, and she hasn't laughed much since we got here.

"Your dad is a computer nerd, kiddo. No matter what your uncle says, this is a good thing. Your dad and his friends help cities run, the stock market operate, and our car work. Nerds rock."

She high-fives me.

"I know that but he..."

"Just ignore him. We live hundreds of miles from

where Stephen and the girls live. When we leave here, we don't have to see them again for a long, long time."

"But Nana said she wanted everyone together."

"She meant to visit, not full time. Would you like to live in Nebraska full time?"

"No way. It's too boring and all my friends live in Seattle."

"Me, too."

Mom screws the top back on the sunblock tube and sighs. "Mary Beth is my sister. I love her, but—"

She stops talking and looks at me. I know she wants to say more but she's thinking I'm still just a kid. Hello, how many times do I have to say it, I'm almost eleven.

"Your dad will be here in a week or so for your birthday. If you want, you can fly back home with him."

I still don't think my uncle and cousins should be here since they weren't here with Nana but Mom's reading her book again, so I just mound up some wet sand and don't say anything.

When Mom and I go back to the house, Rita is sweeping the deck. The way she's stabbing at it with the broom, I worry the planks of the deck are going to go shooting out, torn from the frame.

"Hey, Sis, what's going on?" Mom asks.

"Friggin' sand," Rita says. "Grit gets all over every-thing: the house, the deck, my sheets."

Rita is blocking my path to the door. I scoot to one side, trying to squish around her but Rita moves in the same direction, blocking me. She's still sweeping: stab, stab. Mom moves one of the deck chairs so Rita can reach the corner.

"Better tell me what's going on," Mom says in a low voice.

Rita finally stops the stab sweeping. She points the handle of the broom toward the house.

"Your brother-in-law goes for a run on the beach

with your niece. When he comes back inside, does he take off his shoes? Does he bother to wipe his feet? Oh, hell, no. He and Heather just come tromping across the floor, tracking in sand. I had just dry mopped the floor and there they go spreading sand all over my clean floor. He knows I just swept. I say to him, 'Hey, wipe your feet. I just cleaned.' You know what he said to me?"

Mom starts to answer, but Rita goes right on.

"He says, 'Oops, you missed a spot,' and laughs. He laughs!"

Rita jabs the handle of the broom toward the house again.

"Then, and this really makes me mad, your sister just sits there on the couch doing a crossword puzzle and pretending like none of this is happening."

Mom mutters something to Rita but I'm very quietly taking off my sandals, dusting off my feet, and scooting around them and into the house so I don't hear.

Mary Beth is sitting on the couch, just like my aunt said. She has her hands clasped together and eyes closed like she's praying and she's speaking really low so I can't hear. Riley Rose is beside her, palms together like her mom, but her eyes are open. She sees me, smiles, and gives a little wave. I wave back. I don't see Heather and Sarah, yippee. The door of the room where Mary Beth and Stephen stay is closed but I hear noises behind it. I walk fast to my room before my aunt opens her eyes or Stephen comes out.

Mom told me to take a shower but first I check my room. Heather and Sarah Beth are snoops and I've set traps, so I'll know if they come in. First, I check on my Nintendo. Trap one. It's in the bottom of my suitcase and the suitcase is still under the bed. The trap is a pair of my dirty undershorts that I looped through the suitcase handles. Even if Heather and Sarah Beth open the suitcase, they're not going to retie my dirty shorts back. Second, I yank back the cover and check my bed. When we visited Nana in Nebraska for Christmas, Heather and Sarah Beth dumped snow under my covers.

Picture it. I put on jammies in Nana's cold house and, shivering, squeeze under the covers. I stretch out and my feet bump into ice and wet sheets. Surprise. They told everyone I must have wet the bed the night before. Not! This morning, I pushed the sheets into a secret pattern, so I'd know if anyone messed with the bed. Sweet, no wet splotches, and the DS is safe.

Then I open the bathroom door and see it has exploded with girl stuff. The bathroom Mom and I share is between our room and the brats' room. There's one door that leads to their room and one on the other side that leads to me and Mom's room. I see girly things in bottles and a pink zip pouch taking up the whole sink counter. What I don't see is the cup with my toothpaste, toothbrush, and comb. Mom's stuff is gone, too.

I open the shower curtain—more girl junk in the shower. In the medicine cabinet I find Mom's stuff, but not mine. I look in the drawer where the towels are kept. Nothing but towels and washcloths. I check the other drawer. Still no toothbrush. Then I look under the sink and there it is, the cup with my toothpaste, toothbrush, and comb touching the toilet cleaner bottle. Yuck it.

"Mom," I shout and run out of the room. "Heather and Sarah Beth hid my stuff under the bathroom sink. It has toilet cleaner all over it." A little exaggeration here but I'm so mad.

Everyone turns and stares at me: Mom, Rita, and Stephen who has come out of the bedroom, and Mary Beth.

"What's going on?" Stephen asks.

"Heather and Sarah Beth put my toothbrush and stuff right next to the toilet cleaner. They want me to brush my teeth with cleaning gunk? I hate them."

Mom gives Mary Beth the stink eye.

"There's not much space in that bathroom," Mary Beth says in a whiny voice. "I'm sure they were just trying to make room and didn't realize it was there."

"Your stuff is gone, too," I add to Mom.

Mom's stink eye shoots my aunt, again.

"I don't see why those girls can't put their stuff back in their own room when they're done," Mom says.

Stephen starts to say something, but Mom cuts him off.

"Where are Heather and Sarah Beth, anyway? They can just move their stuff. Now."

To me, she says, "We can get you another toothbrush when we order supplies. Meantime, we'll figure out another way to clean your teeth."

"The Indians chewed twigs to clean their teeth," Stephen says.

"Fine, you can just find your own twig to chew," Mom snaps. "Come on, Henry, you jump in the shower, and I'll make us something for lunch."

CHAPTER NINE

MOM IS LYING ON HER BED WITH A WET WASHCLOTH over her eyes when I get out of the shower.

"Mom," I say softly, but she doesn't reply. My mom is never sick, so her lying there so quiet looks weird and a little scary. Like finding Nana scary. "Mom?" I say louder.

"Oh, sorry, honey. I have a headache and thought I'd lie down for a minute. Must have dozed off. If you're done in the bathroom, I'm going to take a shower. There's a sandwich in the kitchen for you."

Normally, I'd ask what kind she made but I'm still seeing Mom all quiet like Nana Belle in her chair, and I forget.

Riley Rose is on the couch, legs crossed, coloring in a book. My auntie is outside on the deck. Mom fixed me a turkey sandwich and cut it in four triangles, just the way I like it. I take the plate and sit down beside Riley.

"What ya coloring?" I ask her.

She points at my sandwich, and I hand her one of the triangles.

"Kitty cat." She's colored outside the lines in most

places, but I can still see it's—sort of—a brown and white kitten with a collar that Riley colored red.

"Good job," I say after I eat two of the triangles. "Do you have a kitty like that at home?"

"No, here," Riley says. "Kitty here."

"You saw a kitty here on the island?"

"Here," she repeats.

"I haven't seen any cats," I say

Riley just shrugs.

Okay, there's an invisible cat on the island that only Riley Rose can see. I split the third triangle with her and lick the mayonnaise off my fingers.

"Where are your sisters?" I ask. One should always know the location of the enemy. And I'm still mad about the toothbrush thing.

Riley shrugs.

"Are they outside somewhere?" If they're gone, I'm going to enjoy some game time.

"'Xploring," Riley says. She points out the doors, toward the jungle.

Hold the bus. Does that mean the brats are exploring MY jungle? First, the toothbrush. Now my jungle? I tear out of the house.

"Where are Heather and Sarah Beth?" I ask my aunt as I race across the deck. I'm so mad at the thought of those stupid girls in my trees that I can't stand still.

"I don't know," my aunt says. "Last time I saw them they were headed 'round the side of the house. Why? No need to get mad. I'm sure that toothbrush thing was just an accident."

"They went into the trees?"

"Uh, I don't know. Maybe."

"There's snakes in there," I tell her. "Mom told me to stay out."

I'm so angry that I stomp down the deck stairs, leaping past the last two steps. It might not be all bad. A snake biting one of my cousins could be good. A snake-bit person would have to leave the island, right? Better, Stephen would need to go with them. It didn't make me feel better. They have once again stolen something I've already claimed. If my mom won't let me explore, how come they get to?

I stop where the dense trees begin. My heart's thumping so loud I can't hear anything. I look around really fast: no sign of Mom or anyone else. I slip in where the bushes are thinner, moving as silently as a panther through the woods.

It doesn't take long to find Heather and Sarah Beth. They sound like trampling elephants. Make that trumpeting, trampling elephants since they're talking loud enough to scare off any smart snake.

"How much farther do these stupid trees go, anyway?" Sarah Beth whines.

"Shut up and keep going," Heather replies. "Oh, shit, I stepped in… Yuck, what is that?"

I hear sticks crack and more bad words. I hope my aunt hears all the bad words and calls Heather back.

"Mud," says Sarah Beth. "You think this goes all the way to the ocean? We should go back."

"We're not that far. It can't be the ocean already. Come on, we'll go around the mud."

"I don't know. Dad said there are alligators in the marshes around here."

"Crocodiles, not alligators," says Heather.

"Dad said alligators."

This gives me an idea. I spot a big tree branch lying in the leaves. I pick it up and toss it toward where the girls are. It makes a perfect crocodile-tail, slapping noise when it hits the mud near them.

Heather screams. So does Sarah Beth. There's a bunch of thrashing sounds then all is quiet.

Success.

I move away from where they had been. When I think I'm far enough, I slip out of the trees. Then I, as nonchalantly as I can, stroll around the other side of the house, so it looks like I've come from the ferry dock.

Heather and Sarah Beth are on the deck talking to their mom. They're making big gestures with their arms. As I go up the stairs, I listen to what they're saying.

"It was huge, I saw its tail," yelps Sarah Beth. She spreads out her arms showing just how huge it was. "I swear, Mom, it was this big and that wasn't even its head."

My cousins' faces are flushed, and their sweaty hair is stringy. Both have scratches on their bare arms and legs.

"Hey," I say when I reach the top of the steps. "What's going on?"

Heather spins and faces me, fists on hips.

"Where have you been?" she demands.

Wow, is her face red. And splotchy. I try not to grin. It's hard.

"I was down at the ferry dock watching a boat go by. Why?"

Heather spins again, this time facing the ocean. "I don't see a boat," she says.

"It's gone now," I say, shrugging.

Mary Beth gives me the evil eye but doesn't say anything. I'm hoping she was too engrossed in her reading when I took off to see where I went.

"You weren't over there?" asks Sarah Beth pointing toward MY jungle.

"Nope," I say. "Why, what happened?" I bite the inside of my mouth trying not to laugh.

"We were walking through the trees, and we saw

this huge alligator going through the marsh," Sarah Beth says.

"Are you sure it wasn't a crocodile?" I ask, all innocent.

Heather glares at me. It's a scary look with her face still all blotchy and that big honking nose. I go on.

"My mom says there's snakes and stuff in there. I'd stay away if I were you."

"We're not," says Heather.

"Not what?" I ask.

"You."

"A stinky boy," Sarah Beth adds.

Like they should talk.

"Well, why did you hide my toothbrush?" I say, diverting to another topic. "You put it under the sink against the toilet cleaner and stuff. You need to keep your junk in your own room."

"There isn't enough room—" Heather starts to say but I'm still in attack mode.

"There's plenty of room. How would you like it if I threw all your stupid girl crap under the sink, huh?"

"That's enough, all of you," Mary Beth says, struggling to rise from the beach chair.

"Girls, you need to keep your beauty supplies in your own room when you're not using them. There's still three more weeks that we need to share our space with others and then if you want a bigger bathroom, we can just buy a bigger house when we get home. Understand?"

Then my aunt points at me. "Henry, you need to quit scaring your cousins. And all of you, stay out of the damn forest before someone gets eaten, hear?"

I start to deny, but before I can speak, Heather asks her mom in a whiny voice, "So if we buy a bigger house, do I still have to share a bathroom with my sisters? I need my own space."

"Fine, fine," Mary Beth says and waves her book in the air above her. She waddles into the house muttering something I can't hear. Heather and Sarah Beth follow like chicks after a momma duck.

CHAPTER TEN

"I JUST DON'T THINK WE NEED TO KEEP IT ON THE DINING room table, that's all," Rita is telling Mom and Mary Beth a couple days later.

I don't think so either, but I keep quiet. The 'it' is the silver urn holding Nana Belle's ashes smack in the middle of the big table where we eat. Mary Beth had sneaked it onto the table while Rita and Uncle Stephen were busy fixing supper. It had been Rita's day to fix dinner. Since she doesn't know much about cooking, she told Stephen to grill burgers while she sliced tomatoes, lettuce, and onions. The day before yesterday had been Mary Beth's turn to cook and she had also made burgers, chips, and opened a can of baked beans. Fine by me, since grilled burgers and chips are my favorite food next to fried chicken and potatoes with white gravy. Not so for everyone else. Especially, since this was the third burger day this week, that being Rita's choice earlier. Like I said, Rita doesn't know how to cook.

"It's like having Momma sitting down for dinner with us," says Mary Beth.

"I loved Mom, too, but this is just damned creepy," snaps Rita. "What about you, Jen?"

"I think we can find a more appropriate place," my mom says. "I mean, with us eating dinner, knowing what's inside.

Sis," she tells Mary Beth, "if you want her close, you can keep the urn in your room. Right, Rita?"

Rita nods.

Stephen snorts. "Ain't no way Nana Belle's sleeping in our bedroom. I sleep *a la* natural if you don't know."

Everyone's quiet at that. Mom is rubbing her forehead again. I think she's trying to block out the image of a naked Stephen. I know I am.

"Gawd, that's more than I want to know," Rita finally says. Chop, chop goes the knife through the lettuce.

Finally, it's time to eat. Nana Belle is moved to the top of the bookcase. I can still see it from my seat, but that's better than the middle of the table.

After supper, we all help clean up. Then Rita crosses off another day on the calendar with the big red marker. That makes eight days we've been here. More for Mom and me since we came before Nana died but those days don't count. Mom already explained that.

"Anyone up for dominoes?" my mom asks, wiping off the table.

"Again?" grumbles Stephen. "We played dominoes yesterday."

"No, honey," Mary Beth chimes in, "we played Texas Hold 'Em, remember?"

"Oh, right, now I remember. I won. Jeez, how could I forget that?" Stephen grins when he says this. His grin is the one where only one side of his mouth twists up. Smirky, like he knows we didn't play dominos yesterday and he just wants, again, to remind us he won. I've seen Heather grin the same. Like when she tried to hand me her pink makeup bag to carry. Smirky face.

Mom shakes out the bag of dominoes onto the table

and we all help turn them face over. I'd rather be playing on my Nintendo, but my cousins are sitting on the couch reading and they're too nosy. I could just go into my room and play but when I glance at Mom and point to the bedroom, she shakes her head and whispers, "Later." Boring old dominoes it is.

"We still need to decide where to lay Momma to rest," Mary Beth declares when the domino "action" slows. It's my uncle's turn, and he's always so pokey. Stephen will wait until it's his move then—every time—count on his fingers several times before slapping his domino down.

"Seems to me, she's resting pretty good over there," Rita says, pointing to the urn sitting on top of the bookshelf.

"You know that's not what I mean," Mary Beth snorts. "I think we need to bury her alongside Dad."

"I thought we already decided that she wouldn't want to spend eternity next to him," Mom says. "I'm sure there's another spot in the same cemetery where we can inter her."

"But it's tradition, burying spouses together. What would people think if they saw that? They got divorced in the afterlife?"

"They would think Mom finally wised up," Rita tells her as she moves around her dominos. "Let the poor woman have a little peace and quiet. Screw what everyone else thinks. Most of Mom's friends have passed on, anyway. You think their ghosts are gonna all get together and gossip?"

Stephen slaps his piece down.

My turn. I hook my domino onto a seven.

"You only have two left, Henry?" Rita asks. "Damn, and I'm holding all the biggies."

She pulls at her lip and then places a domino next to the one I just put down.

"What about Belle's house?" Stephen asks.

"What about it?" Mom and Rita say at the same time.

Mary Beth is concentrating on her move. I suspect she's pretending not to listen.

"I mean, we should probably get it on the market quickly. Otherwise, things are going to go to pot while we're paying the taxes and insurance."

"You mean while us three girls are paying," says Rita.

"Right, that's what I meant. I think I'm well situated to sell it. After all, I'm familiar with the house and the neighborhood. Plus, I know the market for big old houses like what she's got."

"For your usual commission, I suppose," Rita adds.

"Of course. It's not like we can't afford it."

"We?" Mom and Rita ask in unison again.

"You know what I mean, "we" as in Bethie and I."

Aunt Beth puts her domino in place and then gives my uncle a weird look. "I told you before, I don't like being called Bethie."

Mom and Rita exchange a look. Mom makes this little smile, but she hides it by taking a drink of her iced tea. Very interesting.

"I guess we," Rita emphasizes the "we," "can afford to toss you a few bucks in commission if your agency wants to list the house. I say price it low, so we can get it sold quickly."

Mom nods. "Sounds good to me. We can fix the leak in the upstairs bathroom sink, do a couple of other minor repairs and then list it to sell as is."

"I think it would be better to price the house higher," Stephen says. "Hey, we're not in any hurry to sell it, are we?"

"Let me guess, your commission is a percentage of the price, right?" sneers Mom.

"Just do what they say, Stephen," Mary Beth says. "What difference does a couple of thousand make anyway? Her mortgage has been paid off for years so it's all profit. Besides, there's plenty more in the estate to go around. I just think we need more time to think about it before we decide to sell. After all, we grew up in that house."

Rita adds, "And we need to agree whether we want to have Stephen sell it or go with an uninterested party, which I think is best. Whose turn is it, anyway?"

CHAPTER ELEVEN

It's dark when I wake up with my heart beeping real fast and the sheet all twisted around my feet. The nightmare was so real. In it, we're playing dominoes again, but everyone's talking so much that the game is taking forever. Lots of talking, little playing. I want the game done so I can go to my room. We've been playing for hours and hours but we're still just on tens. Dad's at this game, that's the only good thing, but I can't get his attention. "Hey, Dad," I keep saying, but he just goes on talking about selling Nana's house. Then my mom gets one of her headaches and, *POW*, her forehead hits the table right on top of her dominoes. I want to help her, but I can't seem to move.

"Brain cancer," whispers Stephen. He has on one of those white coats like doctors wear and there's an old-timey stethoscope looped around his neck, like in a movie.

"How long, Doctor?" my dad asks Stephen.

"Three weeks, max," Stephen says.

"Home," my mom says, and her face has changed into one of the zombie people with blackened eyes and sharp teeth showing through one rotted cheek.

"She's going on the bookshelf, and we're getting all the money," Heather sings.

I want to kiss my mom but when she puckers her zombie lips, I scream.

That's when I wake up. I can still hear the dream scream in my head. Did I scream in real life? No one has turned on lights to investigate the sound. Mom is snoring softly in the next bed. Moonlight comes in from the window, and I watch Mom for a while, making sure she stays breathing. She does. What if her headaches are brain cancer? I don't want her to die.

I need to pee bad, so I get up and use the bathroom. Then I'm thirsty. Heather and Sarah Beth use the glass beside the sink in the bathroom and their germs are all over it. I know they do because I have seen the pink smudges of Heather's lip-gloss on the rim. No way I'm gonna use it. Yuck, slimy girl spit. Plus, I want orange juice.

I open the fridge door and use the light to find a glass and pour some OJ. The kitchen is dark when I close the door, so I stand there drinking while my forest hunter hearing shifts into hyper-hunter mode.

One last gulp of OJ, then I hear a voice. The sound is coming from a bedroom opposite my side of the great room. It sounds like Riley Rose's voice. Did she have a bad dream, too? I wait, listening, but I can't tell what she's saying. Then the doorknob turns, and her door opens. I can barely make out a short person in light PJ's making her way toward the deck door. Oh, dolphin poop, is she sleepwalking? What if she walks into the ocean and drowns?

"Riley Rose," I say, softly so I don't scare her. "It's me, Henry."

The shape halts. "'Enry?" she says in her little girl voice.

I go to her and squat down so I can see her better in the dark. "Yes, it's Henry. What are you doing up?"

"Kitty," she says and points outside.

"Did you dream of a kitty?" I whisper.

"Kitty, outside," she says. She starts toward the deck door again.

"It's dark outside, Riley. You can't go outside when it's night, you might hurt yourself."

Did I just tell Riley she might get hurt in the dark? This is something my mother would say. How did Mom's voice get in my head?

"I want to see kitty," Riley Rose says in a louder voice.

"Okay, Riley, just use your whisper voice so we won't wake anyone. I'll take you outside and we'll look for your kitty, all right?"

We go out onto the deck. I hear the waves doing their usual thing: going out with a swish and then back in with a soft rattle. I look around, but there is no kitty out here.

"I don't see a kitty, do you? Is it brown and white like you colored in the book?"

"Black," Riley says, and I see her nod in the moonlight.

"Black and white?"

Another nod.

"And it had a red collar on like your picture?" I ask.

This time she shakes her head. Okay, a black and white pretend cat with no collar. I look around the deck again and then peer over the edge. No cat here.

"There," Riley said, pointing toward the tree line, now tall, black, creepy shapes against the light sand.

I don't see anything, but I pretend I do so I can get my cousin back inside.

"Kitty is going back to his home. I bet he's going to

sleep in his nice soft bed. Time for Riley to go back inside to her own bed."

I lead her back inside, and at her bedroom door, she whispers something I can't hear. "What?" I ask, bending down so I can hear her better.

"Nighty-night," she says, and lifts her face to give me a kiss on my chin.

"You, too," I say and kiss her quick on the top of her head. It makes me feel weirdly happy, like being a big brother.

I'm still thirsty, so I get another glass of OJ after I make sure Riley is back in her room. Did my cousin just dream there was a cat? My nightmare seemed so real. Maybe that's what happened to her. I'm not sleepy yet, plus I don't want to have the Mom-brain-cancer-dream again. I go back outside. There is no cat on the deck, no cat in the sand. It's hard to see in the black trees but no way am I going to get any closer. I had tricked Heather and Sarah Beth about there being alligators in there, but I'd seen warnings along the mainland shore about them. There is something monster-creepy about the dense trees, with their spooky hanging moss, even in the daytime. Alligators or not, no way I'd go there in the dark.

The deck circles around the whole beach part of the house and all the way down the side where Nana Belle's room had been. Mary Beth and Stephen have Nana's room now. Riley's room is next, then a bathroom, and then Aunt Rita's room in the back corner.

I sneak around the edge of the house, staying close to the wall. Cat poop, the glass sliding door to my aunt and uncle's room is open. Through the screen, I hear loud snoring. My guess is it's my uncle but, who knows, it could be my aunt. I so don't want to find out who is the snorer. I sneak to the railing, duck and half-walk, half-crawl past their door. Riley's window is open, too, with the screen closed to keep out bugs. Would it keep out a cat? I'm about ready to stand up again and look for signs of a cat when I see something glowing ahead.

It's Riley's cat!. It's a zombie cat with one glowing eye.

I'm not gonna scream. I'm not gonna scream. I can't run, zombies love to chase people. Instead, I crumple myself up against the railing, behind an old flowerpot, as small as I can and freeze.

The glowing cat eye moves, back and forth. It's at my head level so if it's a zombie cat, it's giant. Should I scream and warn everyone what's coming to get them? What would Spiderman do? What would Dad do?

The glow brightens, and in it I see—What is that? I realize what I see is my Aunt Rita's face. She's leaning against the house smoking a cigarette, that's the zombie eye glow. We're safe.

I don't want her to see me, so I stay crouched against the railing. There's a brighter glow, a blue-white. Oh snap, she has her phone on. Rita holds the phone up in the air, all the time looking at the lighted face. What is she doing? She walks to where the deck ends at the corner and aims the phone toward the back where the dock is. Then she faces the jungle, holds up the phone again, and looks at it.

"Goddammit," she says, and the phone goes dark. I realize she's searching in different directions for a cell phone signal. With the cussing, it doesn't take an A student (that would be me) to know she didn't find one.

We had used the blue phone hanging on a wall in the kitchen, but since we came back to the island after Nana died, it hasn't worked. That does not stop my aunt from checking it every day, at least three times.

Rita pushes her cigarette into a plastic bottle and the glow disappears. My leg cramps and I'm trying to figure out how I can get back inside without her seeing me when she turns and goes down the steps to the ground. Dragon breath, it's a bad leg cramp. I quickly limp back to the door and slip inside, wondering if my aunt might run into an alligator, and just who would win that battle.

CHAPTER TWELVE

Roar, roar goes the blender. Uncle Stephen is making his health drink, same as he's done every morning since he got here.

"Good, God," Mom says. "Doesn't the man ever stop annoying people?"

When I open my eyes, she's sitting on the edge of the bed, slipping her feet into flip-flops.

"Go back to sleep if you want to, honey," she tells me. "I'm getting up while the bathroom's free."

I turn to face the wall and pull the pillow over my head. It doesn't help. I can still hear the blender. Now there's a crunching sound to the roar: my uncle adding ice.

Mom shuts the door softly between our bedroom and the bathroom we have to share with the brat cousins. The blender finally stops, so when Mom comes right back into the room she sounds louder.

"Henry, do you know what happened to my shampoo and conditioner? They were in the shower but now I can't find them."

"Heather and Sarah Beth," I mumble from under the pillow.

"What?" Mom lifts the pillow off my head. "I can't hear you."

"Heather and Sarah Beth," I say. "Remember, I told you. They're always messing with our stuff." I sit up, no use trying to sleep now. "They put my toothbrush under the sink, remember." The next I say slowly, so Mom understands, "Right next to the toilet cleaner. They're pigs, taking up all the space."

"Well, crap," my mom says. "I told my sister she needs to tell the girls to put their stuff back in their room when they're done with the bathroom."

I hold out my hand, palm up. Mom said a bad word, which means she owes me 50 cents.

"Hell," she says.

I hold out the other hand, another 50 cents.

"Ya got me," Mom says. "I'll get you a dollar for the curse jar when I get done. First, I need a shower."

She goes back into the bathroom, this time leaving the door open. She opens the cabinet under the sink, moves stuff, and pulls out a couple of bottles. Then she pulls out the cup holding my toothbrush and toothpaste from under the sink.

She looks at me, and says, "Slimy snakeskin."

I nod. "Told you."

After Mom closes the bathroom door, I put on clothes and go into the great room.

Stephen is leaning against the kitchen counter drinking. Today, the drink is something gunky orange with swirls of green.

Rita is marking a big red 'X' through today's date. That makes ten big red 'Xs' on the calendar.

I start to tell her that we're supposed to mark through the day after supper, but she speaks to my uncle.

"Jesus Christ, Stephen. Do you have to run that," Rita glances my way, "freaking thing every damn morning? It's annoying as hell, especially in the middle of the night?"

"Jeez, it's not the middle of the night. Look, the sun is already coming up. I'm ready for a run. Nothing like a little exercise in the early morning. You ought to try it sometime. It'd take some of the grump out of you."

He lifts one leg, plops a sports shoe on the kitchen bar, and stretches over to grab his foot. He's wearing very short, shiny running shorts, and Rita and I avert our eyes away from way too much naked leg.

"Get your damn dirty foot off our clean counter," Rita says. "Did you not learn any manners?"

Apparently, my Aunt Rita has forgotten about the "say a bad word, pay for it" rule. I could get rich here.

Stephen drags his foot off the counter then with his butt facing Rita bends over to touch the floor. Rita fake kicks him right in the short-shorts but Stephen doesn't notice. He takes the last drink, belches loud, and jogs to the deck doors and out.

Rita uncaps the red pen and makes another 'X' on top of the 'X' she made before on the calendar. It is now thick and dark red.

"Sometimes, Henry," Rita says to me, "just getting through the first hour of a day seems as long as the whole day."

I realize when I pull the juice pitcher out of the fridge why Stephen's drink of the day was orange. I pour what's left—three drops—into a glass. Not even a swallow. Worse, he left the empty pitcher in the fridge.

Mary Beth comes out of her bedroom wearing something Mom calls a muumuu. The dress sounds like something a cow would say.

"Every morning that man has to run the blender before the sun even comes up," Rita tells her. "Why?"

Mary Beth shrugs but doesn't say anything.

"Well?" says Rita. "Does he do the same thing when

you're back home or does he just do it here to annoy the hell out of us?"

Another shrug.

"You don't have to put up with that, you know. Not now, with the lottery money."

Shrug number three.

"Mary Beth, are you hearing what I'm saying?"

My aunt has had her muumuu back to Rita but now she turns around and points a finger at Rita's face. "Stephen is my husband, and I'd appreciate you not digging at him. You've never liked him, ever since we got married."

"I never criticize him," Rita says. She crosses her arms and leans against the kitchen island. "I only tell the truth as I see it."

"As I see it," echoes Mary Beth. She says it real snotty-like. Then she points a finger at Rita again. "That's the problem. You only see things from your perspective, don't you? You got yourself a fancy-schmancy law degree and, of course, the rest of the world should see life through your eyeballs. Black and white. Right and wrong. The world according to Rita. Well, the world isn't as clear as that for the rest of us who have to live in it."

Mary Beth does the finger poke again. "In the real world, families have to compromise. You can't just be a dictator. Not that you know anything about living as a family."

Rita winds up getting ready to snap back but just then Mom joins us.

"Hey, what's going on in here? I could hear you arguing in the bathroom." Mom glares at me like I had a part in it. Or because she knows I like listening to people fight. Okay, I do enjoy it a little. Sometimes grownups are way entertaining.

Rita's face is all red, and Mary Beth is, well, she's

just being Mary Beth, all slouchy and grumpy.

Then Mom notices the big, thick, red 'X' on the calendar. She looks at her sisters, first one and then the other.

"Long day already?" she asks into the air between them.

"Doesn't help, it started before dawn," Rita says and glares at Mary Beth.

"Don't complain to me."

"You ready for breakfast, kiddo?" Mom asks me.

She doesn't wait for my answer. Instead, she puts cereal, milk, and a bowl and spoon in front of me. She so knows me, right?

After cereal and apple juice, since Stephen drank all the orange, Heather and Sarah Beth finally creep out from their bear den. Must have been the sound of cereal bowls on the table that woke them. Sarah Beth's hair is all wonky just like her.

"I need to talk to you girls about how you're sharing the bathroom," Mom tells them.

Heather grunts something no one understands.

"You too," Mom says to Sarah Beth. "I said something yesterday to you both, but it didn't seem to help. I know there's not a lot of storage so if you could leave your makeup and hair stuff in your room when you're not using it, it would free up some counter space." She points to me. "I found Henry's toothbrush under the sink. Again."

Heather looks at me and does this snotty face thing no one else can see.

"Why can't Henry put his junk in his room if I have to?" she says, copying her mom in the whiny voice. She does whiny real good.

"Like I said," Mom goes on, "if we clear out the big stuff, there's room for everyone's toothbrushes and other necessities."

"Well, my makeup is a necessity," Sarah Beth snorts.

So true, wonky head. I think it but don't say it.

Mom looks at Mary Beth waiting for her to say something. So do my cousins. Everyone is quiet for a minute.

"Just keep your stuff in your room unless you're using it, okay?" says Mary Beth, finally.

Go Mom.

Time for me to explore the jungle before Heather and Sarah Beth finish breakfast.

"Excuse me, please," I say and escape.

It's still spooky, even in the daylight. I try to stay in the light, the green light coming through the leaves, but I keep tripping over roots and vines—or maybe petrified snakes—that are everywhere on the ground. The dark part of the shade is worse. I hear slithering under the vines. What if one of the vine things is really a big snake and squeezes me so hard my poop shoots out? I try to stay in the green light. Creepy toe buggers.

Finally, the trees thin, and I squirt out into—wait for it—someone's yard. What the puck? I hear voices. Are they serial killers? Pirates?

The voices stop, and I hear hammering. Voices again, but I still can't understand what they're saying. Are they building treasure chests? Or coffins to put killed people in? I slip back into the trees and move stealthily around the edge of a house. Do pirates live in houses? Worse, do serial killers? I'm moving like a panther and then *boom* I slip on one of the slimy roots. I grab a handful of leaves. No use. I'm on my butt on the lawn, torn leaves tight in both hands. It is very quiet.

Big fat snotty fart. I just know I'm dead. The pirates are gonna kill me.

I turn around and there they are: pirate serial killers. They're staring at me, and one of them, oh gooey horse doo-doo, one has a hammer raised. I jump up, ready to escape but he speaks.

"Hey, are you okay?"

The one speaking looks about the same age as my dad. The other is old, with gray hair and he's skinny with brown, wrinkly skin.

I nod.

Assess the situation, that's what my dad always tells me. I assess.

They're both in long shorts, the kind with those button pockets near their knees. They're speaking English instead of pirate, that's good. The younger one puts down the hammer. He has on a T-shirt with a picture of a tongue sticking out. Rolling Stones tour. I know this because my dad has one, too. Old fogey band.

I don't think they're pirates. Still unsure about them being serial killers, but the old guy is smiling now.

"You scared the bejesus out of us. I'm a guessing we're not the only ones surprised. You part of the family staying across the way?"

He waves toward where I fell out of the forest.

"I'm Chuck Taggart, by the way. This here's my son, Alexander. What's your name?"

Hello, mouth, that's two questions. Better move it.

"Henry," I say. I try to make my voice sound like I'm not scared but it still comes out squeaky, like a baby.

"Nice to meet you, Henry, I heard that the Richardsons rented their beach house out for the summer. That must be your family."

I nod.

"Mike, that's one of the ferry pilots who delivers mail and stuff, said it was an older lady and her family."

"That's my Nana Belle," I say. "But she died, and we have to stay here for thirty days, that's what her will says."

Mom told me not to tell anyone that Nana won the

lottery, told me some crazy person might want to kidnap us, so I don't tell them that.

The old man takes off his old hat, says, "I'm sorry to hear about that, son. I never met the lady but still, sorry."

"We thought she just went to sleep out in the beach chair, but she was dead." I swipe at my eyes, remembering Mary Beth pushing on Nana's chest trying to make her come back to life and everyone crying.

"My mom's here. My aunts, Mary Beth and Rita, too. I was having fun, even though Nana is ashes now so she can't enjoy it, but then my Uncle Stephen came and my cousins. They're bratty girls, and they're not very nice to me. They keep hiding my stuff."

What the snap. I can't stop talking. I squeeze my lips together. Alexander and his dad are staring at me like I'm the serial killer pirate.

"Outnumbered, are you?" Mr. Taggart asks.

"A little," I admit.

"Well, if your cousins bug you too much, just come on over. Alex and I are making a few repairs to the house before he has to go back to college. You can help us out."

I nod. I'm thinking they're probably not serial killers. Or pirates.

I help them lift a shutter and hang it on the hinge beside one of the windows. Hurricane shutters, Alex's dad explains.

I look up at the sky, but all I see is one puffy white cloud.

"Just getting prepared, in case," Alex explains. "It's coming on hurricane season, and I'm going back to the university soon, so we're getting things done before I leave."

"Alex is studying to be a doctor," his dad tells me.

"He has a year left of medical school and then on to his internship."

Alex grins. "I'll tell you, Henry, I'm gonna be very, very happy when they hand me my diploma. I'm so tired of studying. And taking finals."

"Yes," I say, counting out in my head the years and years of boring school I have left.

We finish and Alex puts the tools back in the bag. He takes it to a shed painted the same yellow color as the house as a lady comes outside. She has silver hair all braided down her back. She's holding a pitcher in one hand and a stack of plastic cups in the other. All of a sudden, I'm so thirsty I could drink an ocean.

"Looks like this one could use an icy fruit punch," she tells Mr. Taggart.

"This here is Henry," the old man says to the lady. "His family is the one who rented Evelyn Richardson's place."

Mr. Taggart points to the woman. "My wife, Nancy. She makes the best juice punch this side of the Mississippi. I'm a guessing you're about ready for a glass."

I barely hear him because I'm watching Mrs. Taggart pour a red-orange drink into the cup. A couple of ice cubes follow with a plop. My throat is a desert, with bunches of prickly cactuses, and I'm already wondering if I can get two cups.

We're sitting on porch steps and I'm on my second cup when I hear someone say, "Hello."

Is that? No, it can't be.

"Hi ya," says a second voice.

Tyrannosaurus poop, a ginormous glop of runny, stinky poo. It's Heather and Sarah Beth. How the snap did they get here?

Mr. Taggart looks at me and then at Heather and Sarah Beth. He leans over, whispers, "The cousins?"

"Yes," I hiss. I was having fun, and now the day, the

whole month, has lost its happiness, like a balloon popping. I found our neighbors first. Wasn't it me who had to track through the dangerous jungle, step over snakes as big as my dad's arm, and walk through vines that crept around to grab my feet? That is not something girls can do. Yet here the pests are. First, they take my stuff then my new friends.

Not fair, not fair.

Worse, their clothes are still clean and even Heather, who always sweats like the pig she is, is barely wet.

"More company," Mrs. Taggart announces, smiling. She hands glasses to the girls and pours punch into them.

Sarah Beth turns to sneer at me so no one else can see. Heather is staring goggle-eyed at Alex who had taken off his shirt when he sat down on the porch to drink his punch. She's looking at him like he's a little fish and she's the shark.

I'm thinking that Alex feels like a little fish too close to a shark, too, because he says, "You must have found the trail through the trees, huh."

A trail, a trail did he say? I had to fight panthers, strangler vines, ten-foot crocodiles and snakes, and these sissies found a trail?

Heather is still doing the hungry shark thing, so Sarah Beth answers.

"Yeah, there's a wood post on our side and then we saw a path. We just kept following it and came out here."

Heather jabs Sarah Beth with her elbow. Sarah Beth shuts up.

"My name is Heather," she says to Alex in a cutesy girl voice. I wanna gag.

"Jeepers, where's my manners." Mr. Taggart tells them. "I'm Chuck Taggart, this here's my son, Alexander, we just call him Alex, and the lady with the fruit drink is my lovely wife, Nancy. So, you're Heather," he waves a hand at Heather, "and this beautiful girl," he waves again, this time at Sarah Beth, "is—"

"Sarah Beth."

"Alexander," Heather says, rolling his name around her tongue so it comes out slow and mushy.

Gag, gag.

"Hey, just Alex."

"I'm going to be a junior next year," Heather tells him, cocking one hip.

"What?" Alex asks.

"A junior in high school, but the teacher told me I might be able to skip a year since I'm so smart."

More gagging.

"Good for you," Alex says. He takes a step back. I'm thinking because Heather is stinky but maybe he's just trying to escape. I know the feeling, having been hit with the Heather force field before.

"Good stuff, Mom, as usual," Alex says to his mother. "I'm gonna jump in the shower. Nice to meet you girls."

He walks past me, and we fist bump. Quiet-like he says, "Good to meet you, Henry. Come over anytime if you want some guy time. Dad and I'll be here. We could use your help again."

"I'm going to be here for a month," Heather says loudly.

Not really since I already watched Rita mark day ten off the calendar.

"Good for you," says Alex. "It's a pretty island. I'm leaving soon to go back to school. I'll be long gone before you."

"School?" Heather asks Mr. Taggart after Alex goes back into their house.

"Medical school," he answers. "I guess you could say he's a junior, too, since he just has a year left."

Heather smiles, and it's so obvious what she's thinking.

"Does Alexander have a girlfriend?" she asks.

"Angela," says Mrs. Taggart gathering the empty glasses.

"Huh?" Heather gapes, always the smooth one.

Not.

"Angela is Alex's girlfriend. They're both in medical school. We met her at Christmas, a lovely girl."

Heather runs a hand through her flat hair trying to fluff it. A losing battle.

"But she didn't come here with Alexander?"

Heather does the same slow and slushy tongue thing with Alex's name.

"Not this time," Mr. Taggart answers.

Time for me to turn into Sonic and zoom. I go back the way I came, through the jungle fighting giant-toothed crocodiles and blood-sucking insects all the way home. Sonic never takes the sissy path.

Mom's fixing dinner when I get back. We have tacos with beans and rice, with bunches of cheese on mine. Yum.

Afterward, the grownups decide to play dominoes. Again. Click, clack they go. I'm playing one of the old games I brought from home on my DS. Then, like they always do, the clicking slows and the talking gets louder.

Mom always says strange things like, "she would roll over in her grave." Like a dead person can move, especially all bunched up in a coffin. *Uck*, not something I want to think about. Ever. Nana Belle is ashes, so she can't roll, least I hope not, since she's on the bookcase, but Mom's saying it now.

"You know Mom would roll in her grave if she knew how we're still fighting about that damn house. Hell, just let Stephen sell it. Really, what's at stake? We can sell it as it stands and take what we can get. Or fix it up and, maybe, get a couple thousand more. All this arguing for a couple bucks when, really, don't we have enough?"

"It's the principle," Rita explains. "Why does it have to be Stephen who lists it, anyway? We should find someone neutral to sell it. Someone who can more fairly evaluate the property and tell us if it's worth fixing up. What Stephen wants to do," she turns and glares at Mary Beth, "is to list it above market value so he can get a bigger commission. Hell, it'll sit on the market so long the squirrels and raccoons will set up condos inside it and then no one will want it."

Mary Beth opens her mouth to say something but Stephen butts in, "It'll sell high, just watch. After all, Belle won the," he raises his hands, makes quote marks in the air, and talks in an announcer's voice, "the multi-million-dollar lottery. Step right up, ladies and gentlemen. Buy the winner's house, and the good luck will rub right off on you."

Rita snorts.

Mom says, "I say just get rid of the damn thing. None of us, especially Mom, ever had a happy life there. Plus, the plumbing is not going to fix itself."

"Momma would have wanted us to keep it to remember her by," Mary Beth says.

"Mom said she was looking for a condo, remember?" my mom snaps. "On the beach. That sounds like she was saying goodbye to Nebraska winters to me."

"I say take a vote, majority rules," Rita says.

"But Momma said to work together," Mary Beth complains.

Everyone turns to Mary Beth. Mom's giving her the stink eye.

"And look how well that's working," Rita says. She put up a hand. "I vote we get another realtor and list it."

No one else puts up a hand.

"All right then, I vote we have Stephen list it but we price it low and immediately put it on multi-list so any realtor can sell it."

Mom puts up her hand. Now there are two "yes" votes, Mom and Rita.

Mary Beth says in a whiny voice, "I still think we can fix it up and, you know."

Stephen says, "I don't like the idea of immediately putting it on multi-list. Plus, what price are we talking about, anyway?"

"Fine," Rita says. "You want the whole commission. Who votes on what he just said?"

Mary Beth and Stephen both shoot up a hand.

Mom and Rita keep theirs under the tabletop.

"Perfect. Two votes that we get it appraised, list Stephen as the realtor, and immediately put it on multi-list." Rita says. "One vote to do the same only have Stephen listed as the exclusive realtor for, let's say, two weeks."

"Wait," Stephen says. "Mary Beth and I against you and Jen, which makes it a tie."

"Wrong, brother-in-law, you are not an heir. No heir, no vote." Then Rita slams her palm down against the table making the dominos bounce. "Sold, two to one."

"That's just not fair," Stephen tells Mary Beth.

He grabs her arm, but she pulls away.

"Just leave it be," she hisses.

"I don't want to play this stupid game, anyway," Stephen says. He pushes his dominos to the middle of the table and gets up from the chair.

"You can't leave now, honey," Mary Beth pleads. "We're only on the sixes."

"Screw it," he says. "I don't count, apparently, so I don't want to play."

"Let it go," my mom says low to her sister. She glances toward me like she wants me to take Uncle Stephen's place. I act real interested in my game. Mary Beth saves me.

"Sarah Beth, get over here and finish for your dad."

"But, Mom," she whines. She's reading a magazine, but like me, I think she was paying more attention to the grownups.

"Get over here, now, girl."

CHAPTER THIRTEEN

THE NEXT DAY IS THE SAME BORING THING. MY UNCLE'S *whir, whir, crunch, crunch* early in the morning wakes me up. Today he's in short blue shorts with a white stripe down each side. Like usual, he drinks his healthy junk and goes outside for a jog. When he leaves, Aunt Rita makes a big red 'X' on the calendar.

The thing that's not the same as yesterday is that the glass with my toothbrush and toothpaste is still beside the bathroom sink, right where I left them. I remove the single hair I got out of mom's hairbrush that I had wrapped around my toothbrush and connected with a dot of toothpaste to the tube. I did it to make sure the girls haven't touched them. My trap is still intact and my toothbrush safe from whatever icky thing they could have done with it, I brush my teeth and carefully replace the hair. It's a super-spy trick.

Mom makes me toast with peanut butter and grape jelly on top for breakfast. Then I put on my swim trunks, and we play for a while in the water.

Afterward, she makes turkey and cheese sandwiches for lunch. She cuts hers the regular way but mine she cuts into four triangles, the way I like it. Then we go outside on the deck to eat. Heather and Sarah Beth are building something in the sand. Good. I want to get my sandwich done and go over to the Taggarts' house before they do. I keep my spy-eye focused on them. My aunt is out there too, watching the girls.

Someone bangs on the door between the house and the deck. I look through the glass and see Riley Rose holding a bowl with both hands.

"What ya doing, Riley Rose?" Mary Beth asks as she opens the door for her.

"Kitty wants milk," she says.

"What kitty?" my aunt asks, looking around.

Riley Rose puts down the bowl and points to the woods. "In there," she says.

"I don't think there's any kitties on the island," her mom explains.

Riley Rose has such a sad face that I say, "She told me she saw one a couple of nights ago."

"Where?" Mom asks.

"When?" asks Mary Beth.

I think carefully before I answer. Riley Rose might get in trouble if her mom finds out she was going outside at night. Plus, I like Riley. Weird how different she is from Heather and Sarah Beth. I hope she doesn't get sucked into being like them.

"I can't remember exactly," I fudge. "In the evening, I think, when you were playing dominoes."

Riley's shoulders relax a little. Yep, she was worried about getting in trouble.

"You saw this cat?" my aunt asks me.

"Not really. It was disappearing into the trees. I didn't get a good look."

"I doubt there's any damn cats on the island," Mary Beth sniffs.

Riley Rose sticks out her bottom lip, pouting.

"Come on, Riley, I'll help you carry the milk down the stairs, and we can look for a place to set it. Okay?"

That's exactly what I do, tucking the bowl of milk behind the bottom step.

"Tank you," my little cousin says. I tell her she's welcome but first, I peek under the stairs just to make sure. No cat.

"Hold it, Buster," my mom says after I take my plate and glass inside and start out the door to visit the Taggarts. "Today is house cleaning day, remember?"

Frog fart.

"Hmmm, let me imagine that," Heather says. She's come back from her swim and is toweling her hair. "Henry is cleaning the toilet wearing pink rubber gloves. Oh yeah, and an apron with ruffles."

She cocks her hip and puts a fist on it. With her other hand she's making a motion like she's plunging out a toilet. She blinks her eyes, all flirty like. Then she says, "Oh, I just love cleaning crappy toilets."

Sarah Beth giggles.

I hate my cousins.

"And you, young lady," my mom tells Heather, "need to put away all the junk you have scattered on the couch."

Mary Beth opens her mouth to say something, but then she takes in the couch with girl magazines, hair stuff, fingernail polish jars, and a bunch of dirty tissues that I don't want to think about scattered all across it and shuts her mouth.

"Put your stuff away, Heather," she tells her. "And toss the Kleenex. Anyway, didn't I already tell you not to paint your toenails inside? You might spill something, and we'd have to replace the couch."

"Yeah, Heather," I say. I'd seen her clip her toenails when she was sitting on the couch. I don't want to think about her cruddy toenail fungus multiplying between the cushions.

Heather glares at me making me wonder how much of my thoughts fell out of my mouth.

It wasn't a fun afternoon. I'd think I was done, then Rita would point out something else to do. At least it kept Heather and Sarah Beth busy, too, so they didn't have a chance to walk through the woods to see *"Alexander."*

"How come Stephen doesn't have to help?" I ask, halfway through wiping down the fronts of the kitchen cabinets.

"Don't you worry about your uncle," Mary Beth answers. "He has his own projects to do."

"Right," Rita says. "That would be exercising the fish?"

Outside Uncle Stephen is standing in the surf flipping his fishing line in and out of the waves, unaware we're watching him through the windows.

"He has guy things outside that he does," Mary Beth says. "Inside is a woman's responsibility."

Rita puts the back of her gloved hand to her forehead. "Oh my God, I think we just time-traveled back to the fifties. I mean, really?"

Mom's rubbing her temples, another headache. I remember the brain cancer dream. What if she really does have brain cancer? Does a headache mean she has cancer?

Tonight is Rita's turn to cook again. I already know it will be hamburgers on the grill, cooked by Stephen, with potato chips and sliced tomatoes. Am I psychic or what?

"Geez, I should get paid for this," Stephen says later when he brings the cooked burgers inside. "Your night to cook but how hard can it be to open a bag of chips."

"Good God, Stevie," Rita says. "It's almost the

twenty-first century. Get with it. Women have more important things to do now than learn to cook, like running a country. Quit being such a misogynist."

I shoot Mom a "what does that mean" look but she mouths "later."

"Well, someone has to do it," Stephen says. "The Bible says that women are helpmates to their husbands. Isn't that right, honey?" The last he says to Mary Beth, who's trying to look busy as she lays out plates and silverware on the counter.

"Maybe, if you learned some housekeeping skills, you could find a husband," Stephen shoots at Rita.

"You're a freaking idiot," Rita says. She jabs a finger at Mary Beth. "And you, dear sister, could do just fine without this idiot. I'm going for a walk."

"Good riddance to bad rubbish," Stephen says as he loads up his burger. "I don't know why you let your sister boss everyone around like that."

"That's just Rita being Rita," Mary Beth tries to say, but Stephen runs right over her words.

"Well, I don't think she deserves a whole third of Belle's estate. I mean, she's a lawyer" He makes the hand quote marks around the word 'lawyer.' "And it's just her. We have a family to support and college costs for the girls in a few years. Oh, yeah, and don't forget who took care of Belle. Not Rita or Jen."

He points an elbow at my mom, "Not saying, Sis, that you didn't offer to help but, hey, you were a long way away and busy with your own family."

"Mom's will was clear," my mom tells Stephen, her teeth gritted. "One-third of the estate to each daughter. That is exactly what we intend to do. Right, Mary Beth?"

Mary Beth has her mouth wrapped around a burger, but she nods.

Mom picks up her plate. "Come on, Henry, it's a

beautiful evening outside. Let's take our burgers outside to eat."

We do.

No dominos tonight, a good thing.

CHAPTER FOURTEEN

I'M DREAMING. COURSE, I DON'T KNOW THAT WHEN I'M inside the dream world. Dad's here. We're catching waves on boogie boards and riding them all the way to the beach. Mom is on the beach waving at us. She's dressed in one of those oldie swimsuits, the ugly kind with a baggy skirt like Nana Belle wore. I'm wondering why Mom is wearing Nana's suit when Dad screams. I look around, trying to find him, but now I'm inside a thick fog. Below are dark shapes moving in the water. Dad screams again somewhere in the fog and then I'm awake, the scream still echoing.

There's another scream. What the turkey? I'm in my bed, in the dark bedroom. Mom is in the other bed, but she's getting up. I hear feet pounding and everyone talking at once.

"Heather or Sarah Beth," Mom says, quickly belting her robe.

My brain is still in the dream world, so I don't understand why Heather and Sarah Beth are hurting my dad.

Mom races out the bedroom door. I follow.

Everyone: Rita, Mary Beth, Stephen, Mom are crowded into Heather and Sarah Beth's room.

Sarah Beth is in the middle of the room, hands over her mouth. Above them, her eyes are wide. Heather's mouth is flapping away.

"Glowing eyes. The monster had glowing eyes." Heather points to an open window. "It was trying to kill me. Trying to get inside."

Sarah Beth says something, but her hands are still over her mouth, so no one understands.

Stephen yells, "Slow down, Gawd damn it. Just tell me what happened."

"I heard, I heard, I heard..." Heather's panting now.

"Get me a bag or something," Stephen orders Mary Beth. "She's hyperventilating again."

Heather bends over, gasping.

"Sit down before you pass out, baby," Rita commands.

Heather sits.

"Damn it, what happened, Sarah?" Stephen asks.

Sarah Beth starts to say something, realizes she still has hands over her mouth, and pulls them away.

"I heard a noise, scratching, something like that, outside the window." She points to the window again. Below the window is Heather's bed looking like she pulled both the covers and the mattress off trying to get away.

"I poked Heather, so she'd wake up. Then I turned on the flashlight and, and—" She covers her mouth again.

"Take your hands off your face and spit it out, girl."

"A face, I saw a big face and giant glowing eyes. We screamed."

"Demon eyes," Heather cries, still breathing hard, but not as much as before.

"Ghost eyes," says Sarah Beth.

This is getting good. I wish I'd thought about

scaring them through the window. It's something to remember for later.

Mom's watching me, and she shakes her head. That's when I realize I'm grinning.

"You have something to do with this?" Stephen asks me.

Dang, he must have seen my grin, too.

"No," I say. Snap, it's hard to stop smiling.

"He didn't," Mom says. "He was sleeping when the screams woke me."

"Maybe, he was fake sleeping," Stephen claims, crossing his arms.

"He wasn't," Mom snaps right back.

Go Mom.

Mary Beth comes back with a plastic grocery sack.

"I couldn't find a paper one," she says, out of breath.

"She's okay now," Stephen says. "I'm going outside to look. Gimme the flashlight, Sarah Beth."

Sarah Beth hands the flashlight to her dad then goes to her mom. Mary Beth lifts an arm and Sarah Beth burrows under it.

"You okay, honey?" Mary Beth asks Heather.

Heather is breathing normally again, but she's still sitting cross-legged on the floor. She scoots over and wraps her arms around my aunt's knees. Mary Beth pats her on the head with the hand not stuck to Sarah Beth.

"Mommy?" a little voice says, and I see Riley Rose come join her mom, attaching herself like yet another moon to Jupiter.

"It's okay, Sweetie, your sisters just had a bad dream."

"It wasn't a dream," Sarah Beth pouts.

"It was a glowing-eyed ghost looking in my window," Heather says.

"And scratching trying to get in." Sarah Beth adds.

"It's Nana Belle's ghost," Heather shouts and starts the heavy breathing again.

"Hush now. You know your nana's ghost wouldn't scare you like that. She loved you."

"You didn't see it, Mom. It was scary."

"No such thing as ghosts," my mom tells her. She's picking up the pillow that fell on the floor during Heather's escape.

I'm not so sure about that. Hello, I watch "Ghost Hunters," you know.

"Don't scare your little sister," Mary Beth tells Heather.

Rita is examining the window screen.

"See anything?" Mom asks.

"Nothing. These old aluminum screens. Even if I could see claw marks, who knows how long they've been there."

Rita is talking to us with her back to the window. I see a glow outside. Is it dawn already? Time is always jumbled when I wake in the night, so I don't know what time it is. The glow brightens, and I see something else; something fuzzy moving along the bottom of the window. It rises and now it looks like hair. Like Nana Belle's frizzy hair drifting in the breeze. Like it did when we found her dead. It's still rising. Holy ghosts.

Rita stops talking.

"What?" she asks, but we are staring past her out the window and don't answer.

That's when she turns to see, screams, and jumps back falling over Heather's bedding.

My heart is beeping fast, but I can't pull my eyes away. I see, a forehead, maybe. Then there are eyebrows. It's illuminated all creepy and alien, like Jack in "The Shining."

Heather screams so loud my ears hurt.

"Damn it, Stephen," Mary Beth shouts. "Stop that shit, now."

The light moves away, Stephen's face appears in the window, and reality returns.

"Just having some fun," he says.

Rita shouts, "You stupid fool," and stomps back to her bedroom.

"Come on everyone," Mom says. "Enough for one night. Time to go back to bed."

"I don't see anything out here," Stephen says from outside. "I think you two girls just have a vivid imagination. Have you two been telling each other ghost stories?"

"It was real," says Sarah Beth. "We both saw it."

"Party over," my mom says, pushing me out of the room.

I'm sitting on the couch in the darkened great room waiting for my cousins and Mom to use the bathroom before going back to bed. There are no blinds on the doors and windows on this side of the house since the only thing that can see inside are fish jumping out of the sea. And really, do fish care what goes on in people's houses? Even if they do, it's not like we're watching any fish TV news to know that.

There's a half-moon showing, enough that I can see flickers of silver as moonlight reflects off a cresting wave. That's different from glowing eyes, which is what I'm looking for in the night. Part of me wants to see the ghost. Is it Nana Belle? The other part of me does not want to see any glowing eyeballs. In my hand is a flashlight but I don't turn it on, at least not yet.

The house is quiet except once in a while I hear a toilet flush. I'm watching, watching. My eyelids feel so heavy. I'm thinking I'll close them, just for a minute, when I hear a door creak.

I'm very awake now.

It's Riley Rose. I know that because I hear the soft patty-pat of her feet.

"Riley Rose," I whisper so I don't scare her, or wake up Mom.

"'Enry?"

"Yes, what are you doing up?"

"I wanna see kitty."

That kitty thing. Again.

She goes over to the door and tries to open it.

"No, Riley, your dad said no going outside at night."

"My kitty."

"I'll help you look in the morning, okay? You need to go back to bed before your dad finds you out here."

She bows her head and I know, even in the dark, that she's sticking her lip out in a pout.

"I promise, okay? I'm going to stay out here 'till you're back in bed so you'd better go."

Head still down, lip pouted, she pat-pats back to her room. I get up and watch until I hear the click of her bedroom door shutting.

Then I go back to the couch and think really hard. A cat only Riley Rose has seen, something scratching on a window screen, and eyes that glow when caught in the beam of a flashlight. Could it be a cat?

I think some more and wonder about the bowl of milk that I slid under the porch step. If the milk is gone, does that mean Riley's cat is real? Could some other night animal be drinking the milk? Do monsters with glowing eyes drink milk? How fast would it evaporate?

I want to take the flashlight and go outside to see if the milk is gone, but it's still dark and even though I know it was Stephen, not Jack from the scary movie, I'm still not sure about that ghost thing. I remember Nana Belle's ashes. What if?

I still have the flashlight. Quickly, I turn it on and beam it at the shelf where Nana's urn and its ashes rest.

Good, still there. I turn the light off. Turn it on again. Is her urn in the same place it was before, or has it moved? I shoot the beam at the urn again. I can't really tell but—

I walk very fast, back to the bedroom.

"You still up?" Mom says from her bed.

I nod in the dark.

"Mom?" I ask, and I'm embarrassed how my voice comes out sounding like a baby.

I hear the rustle of a blanket.

"Come on over, kiddo," she says, and I crawl in beside her. Just for a little while, I think, and then I'm asleep.

CHAPTER FIFTEEN

EARLY NEXT MORNING, EVEN BEFORE STEPHEN WAKES everyone making his noisy morning drink, I quietly open the door to the deck. Then, just as quietly, I sneak down the deck steps to the bowl of milk Riley and I had slipped under the edge of the last step. The bowl is still there. The milk is gone.

Creeps. There is a cat…or something that likes milk. I aim the beam of the flashlight under the stairs and deck, but I don't see anything, which is good, since I don't really want to find any glowing eyes, even in the daytime.

Some beast wandering around at night and drinking milk is a secret I want to keep for a while.

I want to leave early so I can see if Mr. Taggart and Alex need help, but Mom corners me.

"Morning, Henry. You're up early," Mom says.

I shrug.

"What's that?" she asks and points to what I'm holding.

"Just a flashlight."

Mom gives me the look, the one where I know she's picking through my brain to see what I'm thinking. I fold.

"I just wanted to see what's under the house."

"And?"

"Nuttin'," which is true, since I didn't really see Riley's cat, or anything else glow-eyed.

"Just put the flashlight back where you found it in case we need it again," is all she says.

Mom fixes me peanut butter and jelly toast for breakfast, again. I like it with grape jelly better than strawberry, but it's still good.

Stephen comes back from his morning run while I'm eating. His face gets red and sweaty when he exercises. And he's stinky. He's pulling out the stuff he uses for his morning drink: blender, protein powder, frozen juice, ice, and some weird green liquid he keeps in a bottle in the back of the fridge. He puts the blender on the island where I'm sitting and starts dumping it all together.

"I'm telling you, kid," he says to me. "You need to start exercising more, get strong like me. Those damn computer games are not gonna help you win at football."

Yeah, like having a red, sweaty face is better, is what I want to say. I don't say it out loud though.

"Well, maybe not football, you don't have the shoulders for that," Stephen goes on. "Track."

He says it like track is way down on his sports list.

I gulp the last of my milk and take the plate and glass to the sink. I need to get out of here before Heather and Sarah Beth know I'm leaving.

"What stinks," Rita says coming into the kitchen. She's holding her nose. "Oh, never mind, I figured it out."

"Whine, whine, whine," Stephen says. "First you gripe because you say I make my drink too early. I decided to exercise first and then make it so you can get your beauty sleep, not that it helps much. Still, you whine."

"Can't you take a damn shower first, so you won't stink up the whole house?"

"Witch," Stephen says and punches the blender start button.

Rita uncaps the marker and makes a big dark 'X' through day thirteen.

I'm out the door at the speed of light.

I find the post and the path through the woods. This way is faster, and I won't have to fight the saber-toothed tigers sneaking around in the jungle.

I don't see anyone in the yard, so I knock on the door. "I can help you today," I say to Mr. Taggart when he answers.

"Morning, Henry. I believe we can use some help today, but it's gonna be hard work. You up for that?"

"Yes," I say quickly. Hard work or dealing with Heather and Sarah Beth. Or listening to Rita and Stephen argue. Hello, easy choice.

"Good, come on in. We're just finishing breakfast."

He tells Mrs. Taggart, "Since Alex and Henry are here to help, we're going to wrench my little run-about boat out of the water and clean the hull." He smiles at me. "If it's okay with your folks, Henry, we'll take you out in it for a spin afterward." He winks. "Just so we can test the clean hull."

"My mom will say it's okay," I tell him and nod my head.

Mr. Taggart said it was a little boat, but it looks big. There's a windshield, and behind it is the boat's wheel; a small one like a car instead of a big one like a pirate ship. While Mr. Taggart fills a generator with gas, Alex unties the boat from the side of the dock. On the other side of the boat is another dock going out into the wa-ter. It's like a sandwich with the boat being the cheese in the middle. Between the two docks, near the shore is an open shelter with four corner posts and a flat roof.

Mr. Taggart pulls the cord to start the generator and pushes a button. Rails that were tucked under the shelter's roof between the two decks, sink down until they're underwater. Then Alex uses a rope to guide the boat under the shelter where the rails had been.

After the boat is in place, Mr. Taggart asks me, "You wanna help me raise it, Henry?"

"Yes."

"See the buttons here? One has an arrow pointing up. That raises the rails. The other one points down and lowers the rails. Now, press the up button."

I do. The generator hums, the water swirls, and then I see the boat start to rise.

"Cool jam."

"Good enough," Mr. Taggart says after a minute or so and I stop pushing the button.

Water drips off the bottom of the boat, and I see the part that was under water has green slime on it with barnacle bumps scattered around.

Alex jumps aboard the boat and hooks the chains hanging from the shelter ceiling onto the four rings at the front and back of the boat.

"Keeps the boat secure," he tells me.

Mr. Taggart hands me rubber gloves—not pink, I'm happy to see—and one of his old shirts.

"Put the shirt on over your clothes and tie the tail up so you won't ruin your clothes and put on the gloves."

I do.

"Ready?" he asks.

I am.

We sit on the dock, our legs dangling over the side. I dip the scrubber with the long handle in the pail of water and something that smells like the swimming pool at the rec center back home. Then I scrub the side of the boat. Occasionally, we stop scrubbing so Alex or Mr. Taggart can spray down the hull.

Dip, scrub, scoot down the dock. Repeat. Mr. Taggart tells me he's lived on the island since he retired from being an engineer. Not the kind that drives trains —I think that would have been fun—but the kind who designs city streets and stuff—not as fun. They ask me what I like to do back home in Washington and how I like living in Nana's beach house.

"It'd be better with TV and Internet, but I guess it's all right, except for Heather and Sarah Beth. Riley Rose is okay. She's a baby still."

I tell them more about everyone staying at Nana's house but trying to say why we're still there without saying anything about having to stay a month or Mom loses Nana's lottery money is hard. It's like playing a game where aliens or zombies pop through doors and from behind walls. I have to be alert. I'm glad when Mrs. Taggart tells us lunch is ready and to wash our hands, and I don't have to dodge through any more questions.

Lunch is ham and cheese sandwiches and potato chips. Mr. Taggart and Alex drink beers. Mrs. Taggart and I have lemonade.

"You've been a good helper," Alex says when we go back. "Let's put the boat back in the water and I'll give you a tour, how about that?"

I'm in the driver's seat and Alex is showing me how to move the throttle and wheel when we hear voices.

"You are in so much trouble," Heather says in a very loud voice even though she is just off the dock. It makes us all jump.

Elephant fart, she always ruins my fun. Worse, I didn't even hear her sneak up.

"Hi, Alexander," she says to Alex, switching to her mushy voice.

Heather focuses on me again and *boom*, she's back to loud and grumpy.

"Everyone's looking for you, didn't you hear us shouting? Your mom thinks you fell into the ocean and drowned. If only."

Switch.

"Is this your boat, Alexander? I always wanted to ride in one like this. Of course, there're not many lakes where we live; that's in Nebraska. Are you going someplace? Can I go along? Please?"

I want to gag.

"Your mom's so gonna ground you," Sarah Beth adds.

"Woo-hoo, how bad can that be? I'm already stuck on an island with you, aren't I."

"Guess you'd better scoot on home," Alex tells me. "We'll go for a ride some other day if you're not still in big trouble with your mom."

I scoot. Right before the trees suck me in, I take one last look back. Heather and Sarah Beth have climbed into the boat to stand as close as possible to Alex. I wish had a laser gun to give him so he can blast his way through the zombie cousins before they corner him and suck his brain out.

"Where in the hell have you been, Henry?" Mom demands as I try to sneak back into the house. I was halfway up the deck stairs when I spot her leaning over the rail. I know if she's using bad words, I'm in very big trouble so I don't tell her she owes me fifty cents for the swear word.

"I was helping Mr. Taggart and Alex clean the boat hull. I guess I forgot how late it was; I didn't know. Sorry." My voice sounds whiny, but I can't help it. "Remember, Mom, I told you about them?"

"Yes, but did you mention this morning that's where you were going? Huh? Did you?"

"No, but—"

"No buts, young man. We were looking all over for you. Didn't you hear us yelling for you?"

"No. Sorry."

Mom runs down the stairs, grabs me, and gives me a big hug. I can barely breathe.

"Sorry, Mom. I really didn't know it was so late." Mom starts to cry. I sniff a little, but I don't cry.

She finally lets me go and wipes her face on a sleeve.

"First, young man, I want to meet our neighbors before you spend any more time over there. Second, if you take off again without letting me know where you're going, you're going to be grounded until you're thirty. Understand?"

I nod.

"Sorry," I say again. I mean it, too.

"Where the frick have you been, kid?" Stephen asks when we go into the house. "Thought you'd drowned. Do you realize what you put Jen through?"

He's all stretched out on the couch reading a book, so I don't think he was very worried. Riley Rose is sitting at his feet, coloring.

"It's been handled," my mom tells him.

"I think you need a good smacking, if you ask me," Stephen says.

"I said it's been handled, Stephen."

"Well, what do you have to say, kid? Where in the sand hill were you?"

"Stephen," Mom warns and she's rubbing her head again.

I feel really bad now for making her worry and giving her a headache.

"Heather and Sarah Beth went over there, too," I tell

Stephen. "I think Alex is going to take them out in the boat."

"Alex, that's the old man's name?"

"No, Alex is his son. He's in college to be a doctor."

Stephen narrows his eyes, and there are a couple beats of silence.

"And this Alex guy is taking my daughters out on a boat to the middle of nowhere? Alone?"

I'm getting an idea on how to get back against Heather and Sarah Beth for stealing my friends.

"Alex and Heather like each other," I say, all innocent-like. "I think they want Sarah Beth to stay there while Alex shows Heather how to drive the boat."

Mom shoots me a look but doesn't say anything.

"I'll just see about that," Stephen says and gets up from the couch.

Before he can slip on his shoes, there's a knock at the deck door. It's Mr. Taggart. Behind him are Heather and Sarah Beth, not looking happy.

"Thought I'd come by and say howdy to our new neighbors," Mr. Taggart says. "And bring these wanderers home."

The grown-ups do their introductions. Stephen still looks mad but not as much as before. Sarah Beth stays beside Mr. Taggart, but Heather glares as she passes me on the way to her bedroom. Like that's new.

They talk some more like grownups do. I get a Dr. Pepper out of the fridge.

"Guess I'd better get back," Mr. Taggart finally says. "Oh, and Henry." He pulls something from the side pocket of his shorts. "You earned this. That was hard work scraping the boat and I appreciate you helping me and Alex out."

He hands me twenty dollars.

"Thank you," I say, and I really, really mean it.

Heather stays in her room until Mom calls everyone

to dinner. Sarah Beth talks a lot about Alex. Oh, he's so cute, he's going to be a doctor, he knows how to drive a boat. Yap, yap, yap, yawn.

She only shuts up when Heather comes out of her room.

Mom's made another of my favorites for supper: burrito casserole. Really, anything Mom makes is my favorite. Except for broiled fish. Hello, that's why fish sticks were invented.

CHAPTER SIXTEEN

"You're sticking around here today," my mom tells me. "Consider it your punishment for scaring the 'you know what' outta me yesterday."

"But, Mom—"

"But nothing, Henry. Build a sandcastle or a sand sea monster, read a book, do one of your video games, whatever. You're staying in my sight, understand?"

"But–"

"This is not something open to discussion, Henry James Rowley."

A sandcastle, how babyish. But I know when she uses my whole name that saying anything more will just make it worse. What's worse than one day being grounded? Two days.

She makes me a fried egg sandwich for breakfast with toast and lots of mayonnaise. I would think that fixing my next-to-favorite breakfast means she's sorry for grounding me, but she puts a bunch of lettuce on it so that makes things even.

"What else do we need?" Rita asks.

Mom and my aunties are at the dining table making a grocery list. Rita had put out the flag on the dock earlier in the morning, a signal the ferryman needs to stop.

Mary Beth answers, "Bread, eggs, chips, lunch meat, cleaning supplies, milk, and juice. I can't think of anything else."

Mom says, "Put down a cake mix, vanilla, cocoa, and powdered sugar. And don't forget the birthday candles."

My wolf ears swivel in their direction.

Mom smiles at me. "You didn't forget your birthday is next week, did you, Henry?"

I didn't forget, well not completely, just that time seems to have warped since we got here.

"That will make you ten, right?" Rita asks.

"Eleven."

"Wow, are you sure?"

I nod big time. I think my aunt is teasing.

"I'm almost old enough to drive," I say.

Mom laughs. "Not for a few more years. I'm thinking that's your dad's job, teaching you to drive."

I like it when Mom laughs. That means she's not mad at me anymore. It means tomorrow I can help Mr. Taggart and Alex again.

Stephen comes out of the bedroom drying his hair with a towel. "Good, still working on the list. I need some things, too."

"Like what?" Rita asks in an unfriendly voice. "We already drew up the menu for the next fifteen days and wrote down everything we need."

"I gotta have that dried greens powder." He snaps his fingers at Mary Beth. "What's that stuff called? I can never remember. You know the one I mean. Just write it on the list."

"You mean the stuff that's supposed to improve your memory?" Mom asks.

"Don't get flippy, sister," he says and flicks the towel at Mom.

"Sister-in-law. There's a definite difference."

"Just write it down," he commands my aunt, who sighs, and takes the list from Rita. "And don't forget the protein powder, the one made from whey, and extra juices. I like orange best, the kind without the pulp. Seems like every time I go to the fridge the juice pitcher is empty."

He looks directly at me, and my half-drank glass of OJ.

"Henry's not the only one drinking it," Mom snaps. "Your girls do their share, too."

Heather and Sarah Beth are still in their bedroom. I know that because I can hear their hairdryer going through the closed door, so everyone focuses on Riley Rose sitting beside her mom with cereal and, of course, OJ.

"Yummy," she says and rubs her tummy when she notices everyone looking at her.

"Jesus Christ, Riley," her dad complains. "Pick up your crayons off the floor when you're done with them, can't you?"

Riley Rose makes a sad face and leans into her mom.

"Enough!" Mary Beth snaps.

"You know what else we need? A couple of those little televisions and DVD players," he adds, "And a dozen or so movies. Damn, it's so boring around here. Some entertainment would be nice."

"And who's paying for all that?" Rita asks.

"I thought you guys were splitting the expenses. One-third each."

"We are, but we pay for our own personal stuff," Mom tells him.

"Well, aren't you a stingy millionaire."

Rita joins in. "Remember, Stephen, the estate doesn't settle until after our month together is done. In other words, no money until after we get back."

"That is, if we're still together after a month and don't kill each other first," Mom says under her breath.

"Nuttin' stopping you from leaving, you know," he says. "Not like Peter doesn't make money from whatever computer thing that he does. Plus, you're a teacher. It's me and my family that has the hardships."

"Stephen," Mary Beth warns in a low voice.

"The only one who needs to leave is you," Rita tells Stephen. "You're the irritant. Plus, we don't need you here, it's my sisters and I who have to stay."

"Well, screw you and the horse you rode in on," Stephen says, and stomps out of the house.

"Sorry," Mary Beth mumbles.

"You don't have anything to apologize for," Mom tells her. "He's the one flapping his big mouth."

"Except you're the one who married him," Rita adds.

"He wasn't—" Mary Beth starts to say, but Mom puts up her hand like a stop sign.

Then she says to me, "Henry, you done eating yet?"

"I'm done," I say and hop off the barstool so I can put my plate in the sink.

"Why don't you take Riley Rose and go outside so your aunties and I can talk, okay?"

I hate it when grownups send me away just when things get interesting.

"Help your little cousin find some shells or something."

Riley is all smiley and bouncing around, so I say, "Come on Riley, want to make a sea monster out of sand?"

Riley Rose is an okay cousin, I guess. I take a shovel and bucket down to the water with me. We scoop and move wet sand from the beach to close by the tide line. Riley collects shells in her little pink, plastic bucket.

Finally, after lots of trips, I look at the piles of sand.

A big mound sits high on the shore and thinner piles snake back toward the water.

"This is the head," I tell Riley pointing at the first mound. "And this is going to be the body," indicating the big pile in the middle, "and that's the tail. Like it's coming out of the water, see?"

Riley nods and pours her bucket of shells on the sea monster's back.

"No, no, Riley. Don't put the shells there."

She smiles at me, then uses her hands to scoop the shells off leaving a hole where the spine is supposed to be.

Aghhh.

I dig more sand and pour it into a separate, smaller mound.

"Okay, Riley, this one is for you. Wanna make a sandcastle for your Barbie?"

Big head nod.

I show her how to pack the wet sand into her pail and turn it upside down. My monster waits while we make the four turret corners of a castle.

Voices make me turn. Heather and Sarah Beth are coming down the steps to the beach in their swimsuits. At first, I think they're going to come down and bother me. That's bad, but then I see them head toward the marker post and the path that leads to the Taggart's house. This is worse, really worse.

I look at Riley patting the sand, and back to see the girls disappear into the trees.

"Hey," I shout. "You're not supposed to go over there today."

They pop back out.

"That's you, cuz," Sarah Beth says. "We're not the ones grounded."

"Henry's a bad, bad boy," Heather mocks.

They disappear again, their loud laughter the only thing left behind.

"You stink," I yell. "You stink so bad that…that—" I'm so mad, I can't even think of anything fetid enough.

Kick, kick, and the sand I had gathered for the sea monster goes flying back toward the sea. I stomp down to where the waves lap and kick the water, sending a spray into the air.

"'Enry mad?"

Riley stands all quiet-like, holding her pail, sand coating her arms and legs. A tear trail runs down one sandy cheek.

"I'm not mad at you, Riley," I say, my anger disappearing. "Your sisters are brats."

Riley nods. "Heather stinky."

It's so funny when she says it standing there on chubby legs, and all frosted with sand that I start to laugh.

"Stinky like rotten dinosaur eggs," I say.

Riley Rose giggles.

"Like rotten dinosaur eggs with poo on them"

She giggles harder and drops her pail.

I help Riley finish the rest of her castle, using the little clamshells she found for the windows and the big speckled one for the top. I'm thinking how I'm going to do the sea monster when Mom leans over the porch rail and shouts.

"Time for lunch, you two."

Mom and I eat lunch, chicken salad sandwiches she cuts into triangles for Riley and me, and corn chips. The chips are crumbly since the bag is almost all gone. Rita watches us eat and then fixes her own sandwich. No chips for her. Mary Beth says she's on a diet, so she doesn't fix a sandwich, although I see she grabs a bunch of chips when she goes back to the kitchen for a soda.

"Fix me one while you're in there," Stephen says to my aunt.

She does.

I want to go back and finish my sea monster, but Mom makes me put on more sunscreen and a shirt before I go. Riley stays inside because her mom tells her she has to take a nap.

The sand I piled up has dried and the mounds have spread out so first I pack wet sand in a metal bucket and dump it on top of the piles I made earlier. Riley Rose left her plastic pail and scoop on the beach, and I use the scoop to mold my sea monster. When I'm done it has a snout and body like a crocodile and a snake tail that stops right where the waves wash in. It has four stubby feet that end with flippers—sea monsters use them to swim fast. Pictures of prehistoric crocodiles have a bump at the front of their nose. I shape sand into a bump, but it dries too fast, and the bump keeps going flat.

It's hot, so I lie in the water letting the waves slosh over me for a while, thinking about sea monsters and big trucks with tires like Tonka toys that can drive on the beach. If my dad buys a truck now, when I turn sixteen, it will be old so maybe he'd let me drive it to school. I'd like that. If someone got in my way, I'd run over them, like they do at the Monster Car show Dad took me to one time. I'd have to be careful and only crush the fronts of cars so no one would get hurt. Still—

"Henry!" I hear someone shout.

Mom. She has her camera and a big hat with her.

"I'm here," I say, jumping up from the water.

"Remember, no swimming without me."

"I was just cooling off."

Sea monsters are scaly, so I use one of Riley's

clamshells and press semicircles into its back. Two of the shells I use to make eyes.

The tide is coming in so by the time I'm done with the scaly back, his tail is starting to dissolve. How long will it take for the sea to eat my monster?

I'm still hot. And thirsty. Quickly, I make sure Mom isn't watching and splash back into the ocean to wash off the sand.

"Shower, first, young man," Mom says when I start back to the house for something to drink. "And don't think I didn't see you jump in the water."

The house has an outside shower and I rinse off. The water is cool and feels good after the hot day. I wish we had one at home. I spray my hair and legs and then stick the nozzle in my swim trunks to get the sand out. Tickly cold.

"The girls out there with you?" Stephen asks after I've dried and gone inside.

"Just Riley, earlier," I say.

"Have you seen Heather and Sarah?"

"Nope."

"Where'd the girls go?" he asks Mary Beth. "I saw them leave in their swimsuits. Thought they'd been swimming or sunbathing all this time."

I'm heading to the bedroom to change, and then I stop, take a step back. I know where they went, and it gives me an idea. I take another step back and pivot so I'm facing Stephen.

I say, using my innocent voice, "I saw them earlier going through the woods. I think they were going to see the Taggarts."

"The people from the other side of the island?"

"Yeah, there's Mr. and Mrs. Taggart. And Alex, remember I told you, that's their son. The one in college. Heather and Sarah Beth like him. A lot."

Mom's still outside, but Rita gives me a narrow-eyed look. She looks a lot like my mom when she does that.

Stephen is giving me the squint eye, too. He just looks like Stephen, normal.

"Wasn't Heather wearing that bikini this morning? The one we don't let her wear in public?" he asks Mary Beth, who is in the kitchen slicing an apple for Riley.

"I think, well, I don't remember. We were making the shopping list when they left."

"And she's been over there all this time? With some college boy who probably has something other than books on his mind?"

I say, "I saw Sarah Beth in a swimming suit, too."

Rita is giving me the same look, but I see one side of her mouth twitch up.

"The hell, you say. Well, I'm just gonna pay that Alex a visit. No college boy is going to make moves on my daughters."

I remember how Heather looked at Alex like she was a shark, and he was dinner. I don't tell her dad that.

By the time they come back, I'm in dry clothes and getting a snack out of the fridge. All three of their faces are red and sweaty and none of them look happy. I'm thinking my plan worked.

"You two," Stephen points at Heather and Sarah Beth. "Get some decent clothes on. And you're not sticking your noses out of this house the rest of the day."

"And you and I," he jabs a finger at Mary Beth, "are going outside to have a talk."

I eat my snack—string cheese and the last four Oreo cookies—at the bar beside Riley. Heather and Sarah Beth are arguing in their bedroom. The door is closed so I can't hear everything they say. Rita's still reading on the couch so I can't get closer. Donkey poop. I hear a loud "Alexander" and "first" from

Heather and "don't care" and lots of "I's" from Sarah Beth.

This is too good. I'm thinking I can hear better from the bathroom that joins our bedrooms. I jump down from the barstool.

"Where are you going?" Rita asks.

"I gotta use the restroom."

"Oh, right," she says, but the way she says it makes it sound like she knows what I'm really up to.

I'm just about to the door when Heather stomps out. She's still red and sweaty but now she has on shorts and a T-shirt.

Slam goes the bedroom door.

"Where are you going, brat?" she snarks at me.

"None of your business." Can't a person use the restroom around here without everyone asking about it? Course, now I really do have to go.

Heather and Sarah Beth are in the kitchen making sandwiches when I come back into the great room.

"Excuse me," Sarah Beth tells her sister in a way that tells me she's not really sorry.

"You can just wait. I was here first," Heather says.

"I just need a knife out of the drawer," her sister hisses. "If you didn't have such a wide ass, I could reach it."

"Me, how about yours? Have you looked in the mirror lately, Frog Butt?"

"Yeah, well, like, like—"

Sarah Beth, always the wordy one.

"Can't think of anything now, huh? Must have used up all your words showing off for Alexander," Heather retorts.

"Not my fault Alex likes me better. He tells me I'm a cute pixie."

"I hate you."

"Ditto," says Sarah Beth.

This has worked better than I thought it would.

"What are you grinning about?" Heather asks me. She grabs the plate with my last two Oreos on it as she rounds the bar.

"Hey, that's mine," I say.

"Not now, punk."

"My cookies, Heather. Give 'em back."

She stuffs one in her mouth.

I lunge at her, trying to grab the plate away but she holds it high, out of my reach.

"Yummy," she says, chewing away. She pops my last one in her mouth, the whole cookie. Then she spits it back onto the plate and hands it to me.

"Here ya go, last one."

Sarah Beth snickers.

"That's enough, you two," Rita tells them.

I slap the plate with the slobbered cookie out of Heather's hand and then punch her as hard as I can in the shoulder.

"Ouch!"

"Stop it," my aunt says, grabbing my shoulder to pull me away.

"Yeah, just try and hit me, again," Heather snickers coming toward me. "I'll smack the shit outta you then call the cops, tell them you abused me."

Rita puts out her free hand to stop Heather.

"Stop! Both of you. Now!"

"What's going on?" Mom asks, coming inside.

"Henry hit me," Heather whines rubbing the shoulder I punched.

Again, I can't believe how fast my cousin can change voices—shouting to whinny.

"Henry, what's going on?" Mom asks.

"She started it. She stole my Oreos!"

"You hit first," Heather barks.

Rita explains, "They're both involved. He hit her but

that's because Heather grabbed Henry's cookies, spit one back on the plate, and handed it to him."

"Didn't you teach your boy not to hit girls?" shouts Mary Beth. I hadn't seen her come back inside.

"Well, didn't you teach your daughter not to steal?"

Go Mom.

"Both of you, to your rooms," says Mom.

"Hold it. You don't order my daughters around," commands Mary Beth.

"Good God," says Rita.

"What the freak is going on here?" roars Stephen, pounding through the door and across the floor, always the last one to a fight.

"Nothing," Rita tells him. "Just a little disagreement that got out of hand."

"Just why do you have your hands on my daughter?" he asks my aunt.

Rita lets go of Heather but keeps a hand on my shirt.

"This is why I don't have kids," mutters Rita.

Suddenly, someone screams. Very loud. So loud, I can't tell where it's coming from. Another scream so horrible I swear the walls rattle.

"Stop," Stephen says with hands to ears. He's looking at Sarah Beth, in the kitchen with a butter knife in one raised hand.

All over me, goosebumps pop.

She points, screams again.

Our heads swivel from Sarah Beth to the bookshelf where Nana Belle's ashes sit. The urn is wobbling.

"Holy Mary, Mother of God," says Sarah's mom. "Momma, Momma, is that you? Can you hear me?" She makes the sign of the cross and clasps her hands together in prayer.

Goosebumps pop out on top of my first goosebumps.

"Guys, guys, calm down," Mom says, "All the

screaming and stomping around just shook the shelf and everything, that's all."

Mary Beth is praying, mumbling something under her breath. Her hands are steepled together so tight, her fingers are turning white.

The urn stops wobbling.

"Well, that was the damnedest thing I ever saw," Rita exclaims.

CHAPTER SEVENTEEN

NEXT DAY I'M PLAYING A GAME WHEN THE FERRY TOOTS its horn. We all go down to the dock, except for Mary Beth and Riley Rose. It takes us two trips down to the dock and back up the slope to the house to haul up all the boxes.

Stephen's going through the mail that's been forwarded, separating it into three piles, one for each family, while the rest of us put away the food and supplies.

"Hey, it came," he says and grabs something out of one of the piles.

"What's that?" asks Mary Beth with her head stuck in the fridge, arranging the food on the shelves.

"Just a brochure I ordered."

Mary Beth pops her head back out, "A brochure for what?"

Stephen takes the brochure of whatever it is back to the couch where he flops down, feet up so that he takes up the whole space.

"Well, I've been thinking about a new car." He grins at us. We, of course, are still putting stuff away while he sits.

"Good," Mary Beth says, "I've put over a hundred and fifty thousand miles on the van with all the kids' school activities and stuff. We looking at getting a new van?"

"I'm thinking more about a vehicle for me for work. My Toyota's about done for with all the travel showing houses and stuff. Cardinal rule about selling real estate, you know, gotta have a car that makes the agent look successful."

"The Camry is only three years old, and Toyotas last a long time. I need a van worse, plus it's more than ten years old. How much longer can we pump money into repairs, huh?" Mary Beth points out.

"What kind of vehicle are you looking at?" asks Rita. She says it in a kind of purring voice, not the usual one she uses with Stephen. It reminds me of a cat getting ready to pounce.

He says, "I like those Hummers, especially the H3 Alpha. I haven't decided on a color yet. Red or black, I'm thinking."

"A Hummer!" squeaks Mary Beth with a shocked look.

Aunt Rita pounces, "What are those going for now? Fifty thousand new? Let's see, how many houses will you have to sell to justify that?"

"Hey, my wife and I are having a private conversation here. What business is it of yours anyway? You gotta spend money to make money, do you not understand that?"

I'm wondering how my aunt and uncle could ever expect to have a private conversation with all of us around when my mom pounces.

"So, I'm wondering what is more valuable to you: an ego-boosting Hummer, or the safety of your children in an old van?"

"Jesus H. Christ, I can't say anything without you two jumping into the middle of my business. I'm outta here."

"I don't know why you put up with him?" Rita asks her sister after Stephen takes the brochure into his room and slams the door.

"I think we should get a Camaro, Mom," Heather says. "My friend, Liz—her parents have a hot red one. They took us to the movie in it last year. With the top down. Since I have my license, I can drive to school. Can we?"

"Not a chance," her mom says.

"But Mom, the van is so ugly," Sarah Beth chimes in.

"Outside, both of you, and take Riley Rose. And you," Mary Beth points a finger at Rita, "need to get your nose out of my marriage."

Rita shrugs. "I'm just saying."

"She has a point about the Hummer," Mom tells Mary Beth. "The girls' safety should be you and Stephen's top priority. Plus, you've been complaining about that van always needing repairs. Find yourself a new car, or a van, and then think about letting Stephen buy a car."

"And not a freakin' expensive Hummer," Rita says. "Can you see some businesswoman in a skirt or an older couple trying to climb up into a monster truck to go look at a house? Plus, they ride like the Jeep they are —rough."

"My husband's right that this is our family decision. It has nothing to do with you two."

"I still want a Camaro," Heather nags. She's moved to the door but hasn't gone outside like her mom told her.

"Yeah," agrees Sarah Beth. "We could drive to school together. Mom, that will make things easier since you won't have to drive us, huh?"

"You're not driving with me," Heather snaps at her sister.

"What do you mean?"

"Really? You stole my boyfriend, remember? You're not stealing my car."

"Boyfriend? Who, Alex?"

"Alexander, and you know full well you stole him."

"Did not."

"Did."

"Mom," says Sarah Beth, using the whiny voice.

Did I not say the plan worked out better than I thought? I'm not going to lose my new friends after all. Now, if I can just escape this crazy people house. "Mom?"

"What, son?"

Mom's rubbing her head again.

"Mr. Taggart said he has some things he still needs help with. Can I go?"

"Like what kinds of things?"

Snap, I don't really know. I need to think fast.

"I'm helping him fix the hurricane shutters for his house."

"There's a hurricane coming?" This from Rita.

"No, No, I mean he told me he just likes to be ready, uhm, I mean, since Alex is here to help."

"I hope to hell there's no hurricane coming. I've never been in one...Nebraska has tornadoes and the damn winters in Chicago are hell, but never a—"

"No hurricane," I interrupt Rita, loudly. Mom's worried enough about her brain cancer. Not true, that's just me worried about it. I hope there's no cancer. I wish I'd said something different than helping with hurricane shutters. Mom is still rubbing her head.

"Tell you what, kiddo," she finally says. "Let's put the rest of the supplies away, and I'll walk over there with you and see what they need done."

CHAPTER EIGHTEEN

"I'LL GO WITH YOU," BRATTY HEATHER SAYS THE NEXT morning when I'm on the way to the Taggarts' house. Like that's gonna happen. Least I hope not.

"You're grounded, remember?" I say.

"That was yesterday, snot-nose. Hey, Mom, I can go, right?"

"Me, too," Sarah Beth adds.

Heather spins toward her sister, laser eyes shooting down anything in their path. I'm in the line of fire so, *bam*, I get it. Ouch. I'm thinking those eyes are gonna make Sarah Beth splatter all over the wall. But she just shrugs a shoulder and makes an ugly face at her sister. Guess there's vaccinations for anything, even laser-shooting eyeballs.

"You are NOT going with me," Heather tells her sister.

"Neither one of you are going," their mom says.

I flash a raspberry tongue at my cousins, but they're not paying attention.

"Hey, Henry," Mom says. "Looks like your dad sent you something." She's holding up—yippee, yippee—the new Nintendo game. I love Dad. It's the game that is just out. The one I've been waiting for.

Now, what should I do? Play the new game or go help the Taggarts? I can't decide.

Mom's reading a letter. "Good news, kiddo, your dad will be out in a couple of days for your birthday. What do you think about that?"

What I think is that I really, really want to see my dad. It seems like forever since I saw him and, suddenly, I miss him so much that it makes me feel like crying. I don't, of course, since I'm almost eleven and only babies cry.

"I'll walk with you again to the Taggarts," my mom says. "Nancy said yesterday she'd write out that fruit punch recipe for me. Plus, I need the exercise."

I hurry, rush back to our room, put on my shoes, and hide the new game under my pillow.

"Stay on the path and be careful of crocodiles," I tell Mom as we walk through the jungle.

"I don't think there's crocodiles on this island," she laughs.

"Anaconda snakes?"

"I doubt that either, kiddo, although it is creepy in here with the Spanish moss hanging everywhere."

"If I was a crocodile, I'd live in a place like this."

She laughs. "That I believe. It does have that dank and dark feel."

I want to tell her how it was when I went through the first time, not on the path, but I don't think she'd like to hear that.

"Yuck," she says, brushing something from her shoulder.

She so owes me fifty cents for that word.

"It was just a bug," I tell her.

"Still, yuck."

"A big green one with a hairy face and big fangs," I tease.

"Good thing it's gone then," she says and laughs again.

I'm glad she is laughing. It makes me worry less about brain cancer.

Mr. Taggart and Alex are done with the shutters but after introductions, they explain to my mom that they could use help staining the wood gazebo in the middle of Mrs. Taggart's garden.

"I have an old shirt that I can put over his clothes. That way Henry won't get the waterproofing stain on his good ones."

"That'd be good," Mom says, "although, the way he's growing, the shirt he has on won't fit by the time we get back home."

Then she says it's fine when Alex and his dad ask permission for me to go out in the boat after we're done. She gives me a kiss and tells me to be home by dinner. "Not dark. Dinner," and Mrs. Taggart promises she will watch the time.

Alex uses a ladder to reach the top of the gazebo; Mr. Taggart does the poles holding the top up and the rails. I paint the waterproofing on the lattice panels around the bottom. The stuff is stinky, like oil only thicker and it makes brown speckle splashes on the old shirt Mr. Taggart gave me. I can reach the panels better if I duck-walk around the gazebo, but my legs start getting shaky when I'm only halfway around and I keep having to stop and stretch.

At last, it's done. We clean up and carry the cans and brushes to the garage. Then we sit on the porch and drink iced tea.

Finally, the fun part.

"Grab the rope when I toss it to you," Alex says.

He's pushing the boat away from the dock. Mr. Taggart and I are already on board. I've been on boats before, but this time I'm helping, not just sitting and watching.

Alex jumps aboard, Mr. Taggart starts the engine, and we're off. It's big fun: the wind flips my hair around, and I can feel the roar of the motor through my feet.

We go around the island to our side and I wave at Mom, Rita, and my cousins on the beach. Heather and Sarah Beth yell and run out into the ocean waving their hands high like they want us to pick them up. Mr. Taggart takes the boat in a tight circle, making the water spray over us and we all wave at them. Heather and Sarah Beth are in water past their stomachs now, and they bounce up and down, yell, and wave even harder.

This is so great. I'm grinning so hard my cheeks hurt.

"Bye," I shout back, give one last wave, and then Mr. Taggart pushes the throttle, the engine revs and we head out into deep water.

"This looks good," Alex says after we get out into the sea a ways. I think I can still see our island, barely, but there are other islands, too, so I'm not sure which is ours. The engine idles while Alex stands on the front of the boat looking down into the ocean.

"You ever snorkeled?" Mr. Taggart asks me.

"Bunches," I say. "I do it in the pool all the time and once we went on vacation to California and snorkeled in the ocean."

"Good," he says. "There are life vests under the seat there along with flippers and masks. I'll stay aboard but you and Alex can go in. It's shallower here so you can see the coral beds but stay on the surface. And stay close to my son. Don't wander off. And if I whistle, you come back to the boat, pronto. Not normally sharks out here but I'll keep watch and let you know if one wanders by, understand?"

The water is so clear it's like seeing the coral through glass. At first, it looks like lumps of dark rocks, not brightly colored like in science magazines, but then I see fish dart in and out. No orange Nemo fish, but some have yellow strips or bright shapes on their tails. There's coral that looks like fans with holes, others that look like zombie brains, all round and wrinkly.

I'm counting zombie brains when something brushes my shoulder. Sharks, man-eating sharks with bloody gums and teeth like knives. I thrash around, feeling like giant teeth are chomping my legs. I can't breathe.

"Hey, you okay?" Alex asks, raising the mask off his face.

Reality returns.

"Can't breathe," I pant, pulling the mask away.

"Must have got some water in it. Here, I'll shake it out for you."

He reaches for my mask, but I already have it off and the snorkel tube is turned upside down so water can come out.

"Got it," I say, embarrassed about imagining the shark bite thing.

"Good. What I was going to tell you was I saw a manta ray over there." He points behind where the boat is. "They've had a lot of bad press but long as you don't step on one, they won't bother you."

I already knew that. Hello, the National Geographic channel, but I've never seen one in person. We swim toward where he had seen the ray.

It seems like only two manta rays and a minute later that I hear Mr. Taggart whistle. It sounds funny since my ears are underwater, but I still hear it. When I look up, I'm farther away from the boat.

"We best be getting back," he shouts, "if you want to make your mom's dinner bell."

CHAPTER NINETEEN

Mom seems mad when I get back home, which is weird since they're just setting the table. That means I'm not late for dinner.

Weirder, my cousins are helping set the table and they didn't say anything bad to me about going on the boat when I came inside. Their mom is in the kitchen banging plates and pots around while she's cooking. Rita and Stephen are gone.

I'm telling Mom about the manta rays and the zombie brain coral I found. I did not tell her about the shark attack I imagined, I'm still a little embarrassed about that. All this I say loud enough so that my cousins will know how much fun I had. *Clank, bang* goes the plates and silverware they're placing on the table. *Bang, clank*, go the pots and dishes in the kitchen. No one says a word, not even snotty Heather.

Weird, huh?

I look at my cousins and aunt, and then at Mom. I start to say something, but Mom motions me into our room.

"But you said to be home by supper and it's not supper time yet," I explain when Mom softly closes the door.

"It's not that, Henry."

She takes a big breath. Is this the time she's going to tell me about the brain cancer? What she says is worse.

"I saw Heather playing a DS game when I got out of the shower after swimming. Didn't think much of it, they've been playing their own games since we got here. Then I saw the box and the cellophane wrapping beside it. It was the wrapper around the game Dad sent you."

I nod numbly. That's when I notice the pillow where I had hidden the game is now sitting on top of the blanket in the middle of my bed.

"They stole my game?" I feel like screaming.

"That's what I thought," Mom nodded. "I confronted the girls on where they got it and they said they bought it before we came here. I got mad, my sister got mad at me for grilling them, but they finally admitted it was yours."

"They played it?" I can't believe it. So unfair. Taking the wrapper off a new game is the best part, like opening a Christmas present, even if I already know what's inside.

"But I hid it right here under my pillow," I say and I'm so mad I'm yelling. I grab the pillow—now with their cooties on it—and throw it hard as I can at the wall.

"I know, I'm mad, too, especially knowing they sneaked into our room."

"It's not fair, not fair," I say this loudly and very slow, in case Mom doesn't get it.

"I know, honey, very unfair."

"I hate them. They need to leave, the stealers."

Mom picks up the pillow from the floor where it landed after I threw it at the wall, plumps it, and puts it back on the bed.

"I wish they would leave, too, but who'd watch them

back in Nebraska? Their mom can't leave."

"Their dad can watch them. He can go back home, too."

"I don't think Stephen is gonna leave my sister alone, not with all Nana's dollar signs floating around in the air. He's afraid if he leaves, he can't control things."

I sit at the end of my bed, far away from the cootie pillow, and put my arms and head on my knees. I'd been having so much fun and now the day is like an old, stinky fart that got stuck under a blanket.

There's a tap, tap on the door. "Dinner's ready," Rita announces.

"We're coming."

"Isn't there something you need to say to Henry?" Mom asks Heather when we're all sitting at the table.

"I wasn't the only one," Heather whines. She glares at Sarah Beth.

"Your idea," her sister snarks, spooning mac and cheese onto her plate.

"Shut up, both of you," Mary Beth yells.

Everyone shuts up. That's because Mary Beth never yells, and it surprises everyone.

"So, girls?" Mom asks.

Heather mumbles something.

"Henry can't hear you."

"Sorry."

"Sorry, what?"

"Sorry I played Henry's game, but he should have—"

"That's not good enough." This from Mom.

"Yes, it is," Mary Beth chimes in. "Heather apologized, now let's just get back to dinner."

Mom starts to say something but doesn't.

Heather shoots laser eye beams at me. I raise my eyeball laser shields and think about how I can un-cootie my game.

CHAPTER TWENTY

Day eighteen. That's what Aunt Rita is marking through on the calendar when I open the kitchen cabinet where the cereal is kept. Stephen is already gone. No one else is up yet.

"You ever see where your uncle goes on his morning run?" Rita asks me.

"Behind the house, I guess."

"Hmmm, kind of rocky on that side. Not a place I'd run."

I hadn't thought about it before, but it does seem strange that I never see him running.

"I saw him doing pushups one time, down by the water," I tell her.

"I gotta check this out." My aunt walks down the short hall to the back door. The house is built on a hill, a rocky one, so the downslope on the front side leads out onto a deck on stilts and slopes down to the sand and sea. The back door leads out on the high side straight onto land.

"I can't see anything from here," she says when we step outside. "Let's walk to this side of the house, it's higher."

We do.

"There he is. Quick, around the corner," Rita hisses, slipping around the edge of the house so Stephen can't see us.

We look out from our hiding place, me squatting low, and Rita peering over my head. Stephen is picking up rocks and tossing them. Maybe, he's resting from all that jogging. Pick up a rock, toss it, pick another up, examine the rock, toss. Then he sits on a boulder and uses the one in his hand to scratch something onto the ground. What he's not doing is running.

"This is too good," Rita whispers.

She snorts, I think from trying not to laugh out loud. It is funny watching him not running.

After a couple minutes, I'm tired of squatting and I'm hungry. Just then Stephen gets up, faces away from us, and does jumping jacks.

"Quick, while he can't see us," my aunt says, and we sprint back to the door and inside.

I'm eating my cereal when my uncle comes back. He's using his shirt to wipe his forehead.

"That was a long run," Rita tells him.

"Yep, a solid thirty minutes. I'd guess four or five miles. It's hard to know for sure since I'm not on a track."

"You ran all that time?" she asks. She has her back to my uncle, and she gives me a quick wink.

"Nonstop. It's the best way to get into shape. If I stop, even for a minute, my heart rate slows, and I lose all the benefit."

"Dang," my aunt says. She's still facing me with her back to Stephen and her face is all red and her mouth twisty from trying not to giggle. It's a battle she must be losing because she takes off toward her bedroom.

"Where'd Rita go?" asks Stephen when he finally turns around, cereal bowl in hand.

"To her room, I think."

Then I turn into Sonic and zoom away.

It's a boring day. I ask Mom if I can go see the Taggarts. She says 'no,' that I'm gonna wear out my welcome.

"But they might need my help," I explain.

"No, I said."

Dog poo, then I remember the new DS game. It had taken me an hour after Heather played with it to de-cootie it. First, I used a damp towel to wipe the package off and then blew gently on the chip—no water for sensitive electronics. I closely examined it, blew again. Cootie extermination success.

Mom makes me stop for lunch and outside time. "You're going to take root in that couch if you don't take a break from all that playing." Apparently, she doesn't take alien invasion seriously.

I had seen Heather glare at me when I looked up from playing, but my eyeball anti-laser shields are still up so I don't care. Sarah Beth has been outside all day, doing what I had no idea.

Then, I have an idea where she might be.

Snap, I'm so right. Mom and I are swimming later when I see Sarah Beth come out of the jungle. She has a water bottle and it's filled with something red. It's Mrs. Taggart's special fruit punch.

"Mom," I say and point.

"None of our business," she says and resumes her swim along the beach.

I thought Mary Beth grounded them both.

"Mom," I shout. She stops swimming.

"I gotta go," I say and point down at my bathing trunks and then toward the house. I don't really have to pee since I already did that in the ocean, but I want to find out what Heather says when she sees her sister's bottle of punch. And if she even knows what that means.

Mom waves and resumes swimming.

Riley Rose is coming down the steps when I go up. She has a bowl of milk in both hands. Most of it is sloshing out as she goes slowly down—one step by one step.

"Help, 'Enry," she tells me. I want to see what is going on inside but I'm afraid all the milk will be gone by the time she gets to the bottom.

"Okay, Riley, gimme the bowl and I'll take it down."

I race down, no drops spilling, and slip the bowl under the bottom step. Then I race back up.

Not too late after all.

"That's so unfair," Heather is saying, hands on her hips. She's telling that to her mom, but she's glaring at Sarah Beth. Sarah Beth must still have her anti-laser shield up because she calmly takes a sip of her punch.

"Both of you were supposed to be grounded," their mom says.

"Oh, I thought that was just yesterday." Sarah Beth grins and takes another sip. "I had to help Alex."

This comment doesn't fool me, and it doesn't fool her sister either.

"You little witch," Heather screams and launches at her sister.

This is getting better. I want to tell Heather she owes the curse jar, but I don't think this is the right time.

Heather slaps Sarah Beth. Sarah Beth kicks out at her, misses, kicks again, and connects with Heather's knee.

Heather goes down screaming.

"Ouch, ouch. Mom!"

I hear a knock on the door behind me, Riley Rose. I should help her but can't stop watching my cousins.

"She slapped me," Sarah Beth is saying, holding her cheek.

"You, you broke my knee. Mom!"

Knock, knock.

I slide the door open and let Riley Rose in, but I hold onto her, so she won't get caught up in the fight. I don't really have to since the battle is over. Heather is on the floor crying and holding her knee.

"Alex said to tell you 'Hi.' He's leaving in a couple days," says Sarah Beth as she walks by her sister, taking another sip.

Heather, fast as a snake, grabs Sarah's ankle as she goes by and trips her. The punch bottle flies, hits the ground, the lid pops off, and punch goes everywhere.

"Enough," yells their mom.

"I hate you," Sarah Beth screams, moving fast to rescue what's left of the punch still dribbling out of the bottle.

"I hate you more, toad butt," shouts Heather. She three-legged-crab scoots closer to her sister and knocks the rescued bottle out of Sarah Beth's hand. Again, the bottle bounces, and punch flies.

Sarah Beth throws herself on top of Heather, punching and pulling her hair. Then Heather is on top: slap, punch, hair pull.

Riley Rose wraps her arms around me and buries her head in my side. I pat her on the head but keep my eyes on the fight. I can't stop grinning.

"Stop, stop," shouts their mom. She pulls on Heather's arm but has to shuffle out of the way when they roll toward her.

Only when their dad shouts, "Stop the *F$#)!@* fighting before I smack the crap outta you both!" do they finally stop.

The rest of the afternoon is really quiet. I play on the DS. Heather pouts, a bag of ice on her knee. Sarah Beth is shut in their bedroom. Stephen and Mary Beth are outside talking. Once in a while, I hear their voices, but I don't pay attention since I'm on the hunt for an alien enemy.

CHAPTER TWENTY-ONE

"Your dad will be here soon," Mom tells me that night when she kisses my head and tucks the sheet around my shoulders.

I can't wait.

It takes me a long time to go to sleep thinking about seeing my dad again. Finally, I do, but what seems like a minute later I hear a noise, like a shuffle and the sound of a door closing. It's someone walking down the hall and out the back door.

Riley Rose, going outside. Again. This time, out the back door. Doesn't my little cousin ever sleep? She's going to get hurt. Or lost.

I put on my shoes and follow after her, down the hall and out the door. I know I should wake up her mom and dad, but I don't want to get Riley Rose in trouble.

"Riley?" I whisper when I step outside. It's as dark out here as it was in the bedroom, so my panther eyes have already adjusted to the night. I still don't see Riley.

"Riley Rose, where are you?" This time I whisper louder.

Then I see a glowing point moving toward the dock and the empty boathouse. There are two glows. One, a small red dot moves around. The other I recognize is a flashlight playing back and forth over the ground.

Riley found a flashlight?

Then I realize the red glow is too high to belong to Riley and the figure silhouetted in the reflection of the flashlight is too tall.

The figure stops and I see the red glow lift, brighten, and I understand.

It's Rita, she's the only one who smokes, but what is she doing out here?

I'd seen her before, smoking outside at night, but that's usually on the deck, not out here away from the house at night on rocky ground.

A third glow joins in. That one I know, it's the light from her cellphone. What the turd? I thought there wasn't any service on the island. I know that because it has been making Rita crazy nervous about not being able to "reach out to civilization." That's what she calls it.

The flashlight beam is moving again, back and forth along the ground in front of her.

Panther pupils wide and feet quiet as paws, I follow.

Rita shuffles along the rocky ground until she reaches the dock.

Our boathouse sits between two docks, a short one and a longer one where the ferry stops. The boathouse looks a lot like the one the Taggarts have, a peaked tin roof that rests on top of four corner poles. At the land end is a railing instead of a box that holds a generator like the Taggarts.

Rita must have put out the cigarette because there is only the light from her flashlight now. The beam trails along the top of the roof and then the railing. She turns on the cellphone and holds it up, turning one direction and then another.

I think I know why she's here. She's looking for a

signal. What I don't know is why she decided to look for cell service at night. I wish Dad was already here. I could ask him if the moon affects phone signal reception. My dad is very smart about things like that.

I'm crouching behind a boulder so I can't be seen as I watch. I'm glad I am when Rita sweeps the light around behind her. So, this is a secret she doesn't want anyone to know. Curiouser and curiouser.

She beams the flashlight up along the roofline again, then the light does a wobble, wobble and I can't figure out what's going on. After a minute, I see that my aunt has climbed onto the top of the fence rail. I can't see really well with all the wobbling, but she must have found a ladder or something because now I see her silhouetted on the flat roof, blocking the stars.

Meatballs, I can't believe she actually climbed that high. What is my aunt doing? I want to get closer but I'm afraid she's going to shine the light around again and catch me.

Flash, the cellphone illumination comes on. Rita lifts the phone above her head and moves it around: side-to-side, up and down. She's looking for phone reception, at night while everyone else, except those with panther night vision, is asleep. I'm so going to ask Dad about it.

I hear the beep-beep of a number being dialed. Nothing for a minute. She shakes the phone, the illumination bouncing up and down. I put a hand over my mouth to keep from laughing. Like my aunt doesn't know that shaking a phone doesn't help. Old people, huh.

She holds the phone up again then scoots her way across the top of the shed toward the water. Smack-a-roni, what is she trying to do? My auntie is skinny, but will the roof hold her up? Scoot, scoot; stop to check reception; scoot, scoot; stop and check again. When she gets to the end of the roof, I see the flick of a flame and know she's lighting another cigarette. It's kind of cool the way the stars shine through the smoke.

After a minute or so—she must be done with the cigarette—she checks reception, again holding the phone as high as she can. Then, oh, pooper, I see her trying to stand, all hunchy and stuff. I think she's scared. I don't think I would be scared but, maybe, just a little. Can panthers climb?

Still hunched, she uses both hands to hold the phone high and punch numbers.

My palms are all sweaty just watching and I can't stay still any longer. I stand. At the same time, I hear a little yelp and there goes the phone, clankity clank down the tin roof, and plops onto the deck. Rita waves her hands trying to keep her balance and then she's falling, and I'm running toward her.

Splash she goes into the water—water so black I can't see anything. Then she surfaces all sputtering. Her face bone-pale in the moonlight.

"Aunt Rita, are you okay?" I whisper-yell.

She says a lot of bad words. Some I never heard before, so many that I lose count.

One hand reaches out of the water, and I grab it. After more bad words, me pulling and her straining, she's finally out of the water and sitting on the dock. She's panting and looking funny all wet with her hair plastered down and slimy moss strands on her clothes. She smells bad too, like there was a dead fish down there or something.

"Henry, what are you doing out here?" she hisses. Like she forgot I just saved her life.

"I couldn't sleep," is all I can think to say.

"Hell. Well, I guess I should be grateful you were here."

Yeah, that's what superhero panthers do, you know.

Panthers, superhero or not, don't like water so I'm happy I didn't have to jump in to save her.

My aunt breathes fast for a while, and then slowly goes back to normal. She runs fingers through her wet hair trying to fluff it. I'd seen Heather do the same thing. What is it with girls and their hair, anyway?

"Hey, here's your phone," I say. I thought the plop I heard was it falling in the water, but the phone had landed on the wooden pier.

She clicks it on, inspects it.

"All that shit for nothing. I guess I can be grateful it didn't fall into the water." She stops talking, and I could tell even in the dark that her eyeballs are on me.

"Henry, this is our little secret, okay?"

I shrug. "All right, I guess." Like in the morning anyone would believe this.

"I promise, I'll pay you back for not telling."

Visions of a new bicycle dance in my head.

CHAPTER TWENTY-TWO

TODAY IS MY BIRTHDAY. I STRETCH MY ARMS OVERHEAD so I'm as tall as I can be between fingertips and toes and then stay in bed for a while to see if eleven years old feels different than yesterday's ten.

"Happy Birthday, Henry," Mom says, coming out of the bathroom. She gives me a big hug and a kiss on my head. I decide that hugs and kisses are good, even if I am eleven.

"Do I look bigger?" I ask.

She holds my shoulders and examines me for a long time. Her eyes are all shiny.

"You, young man, are growing way too fast. And," she strokes my cheek, "soon you'll be taller than me and shaving. Then where will my baby boy have gone?"

"I'm not a baby anymore."

She gives me another squeezy hug. "No honey, today you're jumped into the doubles: one, one. Eleven, I can't believe it. Best get up, now. Your dad should be here around noon on the ferry. I have your cake to make, and we need to straighten up the house before he arrives."

I dress fast as Sonic.

I walk out to the very end of the dock, lean out, and

look in the direction the ferry comes. This I do four times in the morning but no ferry. Four times I slump back. Did Dad miss the plane? Did he forget today is my birthday? I check the calendar and recheck it. My aunt has already 'X'ed' through my birthday date. Then I have doubts. Would Rita mark the days ahead to fool us so we can go home early? Is it too soon to check for the ferry again?

"Damn, boy, you're gonna wear out the path to the pier," Stephen tells me.

"I bet your dad forgot," Heather, the snot face, tells me.

"Did not," I say, although I am worried.

"Don't listen to them," Mom tells me. "Here, I made you a sandwich for lunch. It's going to be a while before dinner."

My tummy is too bumpy to eat, so first I squish the bread flat, so the sandwich looks smaller. I take a small bite and then a bigger one. Guess the bumpy feeling was just my tummy telling me it was hungry after all.

"Toot, toot," goes the ferry horn and I run fast as I can out the door and down the path to meet Dad.

I'm jumping up and down as he gets off the boat. He looks around like he can't see me.

"Where's Henry?" he asks my mom when she joins us.

What the fart? I wave my arms. "I'm here, I'm here."

Mom shrugs, "I thought I saw him come down."

"Here I am. Here I am, Dad."

Dad is still looking around.

Dragon snot, Am I invisible? I grab him around the waist. "I'm here."

"Holy meatballs and spaghetti, is this big guy my Henry?" Dad twirls me around. "What has your mom been feeding you? I swear you've grown a foot since I last saw you."

My dad, the jokester. I show him just how big I am by carrying his duffel all the way back to the house. It's heavier than it looks.

After dinner, I'm so full and so happy that all I can do is half-sit, half-lie on the couch with my eyes closed and a ginormous smile on my face. It's because Mom made a great supper—my favorite of chicken, fried and then baked so the skin is all crunchy and yummy; mashed potatoes with lots of cream gravy; and corn on the cob. I had two pieces of corn spread with salt and butter.

It would have been perfect except, when I open my eyes, I can still see Heather and Sarah Beth in the room. They must have made up because they're talking softly together on the other couch and Heather has turned off the laser-eye thing.

The grown-ups, except for Rita, are still at the dinner table. She's at the bar, reading through the newspaper and mail Dad brought over for her.

"So, the president has ordered part of our troops back home?" Stephen asks.

"Yes, about time. The war's gone on longer than anyone expected," my dad says.

"I just love seeing the troops arrive back at base," Mary Beth adds. "Makes me cry every time when the commander releases the soldiers, and their families rush to greet them."

"That's so mushy," Stephen sneers.

"I like to watch it, too," Mom says, "It's a tough job in the middle of a hostile country and being away from their families so long."

"Still mushy," declares Stephen.

"I can't recall, Stephen, did you say you served or didn't serve in the military?" asks my dad.

"Like with the family and my real estate business, I

have time to fight a war?" Stephen whines in a loud voice.

"Hey, no problem, just asking," says my dad. "I was in college when 9/11 happened. Thought about enlisting but well, stuff happened, and I didn't. Anyway, I admire those who put themselves out in front for our country. And I'm always happy to see them come home safe."

I'm still listening when Riley Rose climbs up beside me. "'Appy Birtday, 'Enry," she says and hands a folded paper to me. It has Scotch tape everywhere. There is a crayon drawing of stick flowers on the front and when I turn it over, I see a green outline of a hand, like Riley put her hand down and traced around it with a crayon. Red circles on the tips, I decide, are supposed to be painted fingernails.

"Nice, Riley."

"Open it," she says, and I realize the drawings must be the wrapper and there's something inside.

"You made a present for me?"

Riley nods big. "Open," she says and points to the present.

I carefully pull the tape away. It takes a while because there is tape EVERYWHERE. Riley bounces on the couch like I'm so slow but I don't want to tear it. I open the folded page and inside is another folded paper, this one smaller and thicker.

I unfold the second one, at least there's no tape, and smooth it flat.

"Very pretty."

It's a picture of a big cat face she had torn from her coloring book. Riley colored the cat's face and ears black, mostly staying inside the lines. There is a crooked white stripe on its head, blue eyes, and a little pink nose.

"You did good," I say and mean it. "Is this a picture of your kitty?"

She nods and bounces some more. I gave her a one-armed, side hug.

"Thank you, Riley Rose."

"What is that?" her dad asks Riley.

Riley snatches the drawing and hides it under her leg like she thinks she's going to be in trouble.

"Riley drew a picture for my birthday, a real good one," I say.

The picture reappears from under her leg.

"Let me guess," he says. "Yet another picture of her imaginary cat?"

"I saw it, too," I say. I didn't really, but Riley is looking so sad that I want to protect her.

"You actually saw it?" asks Mary Beth. "Damn, I thought she just imagined it."

"Let me see," Stephen says, waving Riley over to him.

Riley slides off the couch and pad-pads over to show the drawing to her dad.

"So, on a dark night, you saw this black cat, huh?" Stephen asks me.

"It had white on it, too." Behind my back, my fingers are crossed. I avoid looking at Mom. She always knows when I'm telling a lie.

"If my son says he saw a cat then he saw it. Right, son?" Dad says.

I nod. I'm in deep buffalo doodoo. Should I waste my birthday candle wish on the lie about seeing the cat sprout wings and fly away?

"'Enry see kitty."

Riley beams at me with such a happy face that it makes the lie worth it.

Then it's time to open my presents and eat birthday cake. When I blow out the candles on the cake—all eleven in one blow—I decide not to use up my birthday wish on making my lie about seeing the kitty go away. My real wish is, well, I can't say it out loud so I'll just think about this—I can't wait until we're back home again. The cake is white with blue frosting, yummy.

I play my birthday DS game while the grownups play cards. Every once in a while, I peek at the envious Heather and Sarah Beth. Best birthday ever.

CHAPTER TWENTY-THREE

Dad can only stay a couple of days, so we spend the whole next day together. We find boogie boards and life vests in the storage box under the house and ride the waves until we finally collapse on the beach.

"Man, I'm going to have to find time to exercise more," he tells me. "I'm so out of shape even a shark would spit me back out."

He pretends to take a bite out of his arm and spits it out. "Yuck. You, on the other hand…" he grabs my arm and pretends to bite it, "…yummy, muscles."

I laugh and try to pull away, but he keeps me tight, growling and pretending to bite me.

I'm so happy he's here.

Dad tells me about home and that my friend, Jake, keeps asking when I'll be back. I tell him all about helping the Taggarts and going out on the boat. I also tell him how mean Heather and Sarah Beth have been and about how they fought over Alex.

"Girl drama, huh?" he says.

I nod.

"I had two sisters growing up, so I know what you're going through. Girls like to tattle and get us in trouble."

"They stink, too."

"And they spread their makeup and junk all over the bathroom."

Is my dad smart or what?

"Mom is okay though, right?" he asks, "even if she is a girl."

"Mom is not a stinky girl."

"Your mom was never, ever a stinky girl."

We bump fists.

Too, too soon it's time for Dad to go. I hug him so hard he coughs and says, "Help, a constrictor snake got me."

Mom gives him a constrictor hug, too. Then he boards the ferry for home. Mom and I wave until we can no longer see the ferry. She and my dad talked for a long time last night outside on the deck. I wanted to go join them and ask if I could get a puppy when we got home, but instead, I fall asleep on the couch, visions of puppies running across my brain.

"This is all your fault you know," Heather tells Sarah Beth the afternoon after Dad left.

They have appeared at the start of the forest path between Nana Belle's house and the Taggarts'. They're so loud I can hear them from the deck where I had gone with the DS and my new game after Mom told me I needed some outside time.

"Really?" Sarah Beth says. "Like I'm in charge of Alex's life."

"It's Alexander, and you know what I mean, cheese brain."

"You're just jealous 'cause Alex likes me better."

"Jealous, ha! You know I already claimed him."

"What? You're the queen and he's your slave. Is that what you mean?"

"No, it means I saw him first and that means you didn't have any business talking to him."

Sarah Beth stops walking and turns to her sister, hand on one cocked hip.

"Woo-hoo, so now I can't talk to anyone you've staked a claim on. Plus…plus, maybe, he saw me first. How about that? Maybe, you're the boyfriend stealer."

I hit pause on the game. Watching them is more fun.

"I'm the one in high school; you're just a snot baby."

"Yeah, right. Like he'd be interested in some girl in high school when he's surrounded with pretty girls. Plus, he already has a girlfriend, remember?"

"Lard brain."

"Heather is jealous, Heather is jealous," Sarah Beth sings.

Like I haven't seen this movie before.

Heather smacks Sarah Beth across the face, right in mid-song. Sarah Beth springs at Heather and they're down and rolling around in the sand. Heather is on top. Flip, Sarah Beth is on top. They're flailing, screaming and there's a lot of bad words, very loud. It's aliens versus aliens. I'm waiting for green blood to shoot out.

"Stop, right now," Mary Beth yells. I jump, having not heard the deck door open. My aunt can scream for sure.

"Girls, stop fighting," she shouts. "I can't believe you all are fighting. Again."

More noise behind me and now Stephen is pounding down the stairs toward them. He grabs Heather with one hand, Sarah Beth with the other. The girls are still flailing away but nothing is connecting. Then Sarah Beth kicks out and Heather goes down, pulling her dad down with her. Sand flies everywhere.

"What's going on out here?" Rita yells.

"Damn it, not again," my mom says, right behind Rita.

Mary Beth gasps, says, "Oh, Lord Jesus, I'm gonna have a heart attack." She puts a hand on her chest and drops into a chair, her bulk making the deck shake.

"Ah, shit, shit," Rita groans. She leans over the railing and shouts, "Stop the stupid fighting, your mom's having a heart attack."

They stop.

"Idiots," she says and turns to Mom who's helping Mary Beth.

Mom and Rita help my aunt into the house and onto the couch. Rita fans her with a towel while Mom fills a baggie with ice to put on her neck. Riley Rose keeps patting her mom on the leg, whimpering a little.

"Guess I just had the vapors," Mary Beth claims a few minutes later. Rita has turned down the AC and the house is shivery cold. Mary Beth is propped up on the couch, legs up, pillows behind her back, and the ice bag on top of her head. There's a big glass of tea beside her. Stephen is fanning her now. The cause of the trouble— my cousins—are in their room, door shut, shower going.

"Crap. That's all I need now, you having a heart attack," Stephen tells my aunt.

She takes the ice pack off her head and says in a cold voice, "Just what do you mean by 'now'?"

"I mean, well, hell. I mean out here in the middle of nowhere. They'd have to fly in a helicopter to get you out and how would we even call for help?"

She gives him the evil eye.

He shrugs. "I mean if you have to leave the island, then what happens to the money?"

"Really concerned about your wife, aren't you?" Rita says, glaring at Stephen.

"Of course, she's my wife. I'm just saying…"

"Don't say it," Mary Beth warns.

"Jesus H. Christ, I try to help, and everyone misinterprets. I'm taking a shower, there's sand everywhere."

Slam goes his bedroom door.

"Ignore him," Mom says, and pats Mary Beth on the shoulder.

"Damn, it's cold in here. All right if I turn the thermostat back up?" Rita says, shivering.

Mary Beth waves a hand. She looks like she's about ready to cry, but I can't tell for sure since she has unwrapped the towel from around the ice bag and put it over her face.

We have a quiet supper. Mom cooks since Mary Beth is still resting on the couch. Everyone is extra polite the rest of the evening, except for Heather and Sarah Beth. They just glare at each other.

WHIR, WHIR GOES STEPHEN'S BLENDER. *CRUNCH, GRIND,* as he drops in ice cubes. Rita is crossing through day twenty-two on the calendar when I go into the kitchen.

"Eight more days, then I swear I'm going to stomp that damn blender into a million pieces," she tells Stephen.

"Well, good morning and screw you, too," he answers.

"That's fifty cents for the cuss jar," I say, getting a cereal bowl out of the cabinet.

"Listen, little mister smart mouth, I've heard enough from you."

That from the person who did the cursing.

"Don't talk to my son like that," Mom says sharply, entering the battle.

"He needs to shut his fat mouth."

"All I said was—" I begin, but Mom interrupts.

"Stephen, I suggest you worry about your own house. Heather and Sarah are the troublemakers. I'm not sure why you and the girls are here, anyway. If you're not happy, then go home. We don't need you."

Stephen's face is getting all red, like the flimsy running shorts he's wearing. I quickly pour milk over my cereal and scoot around the corner of the kitchen island. Battling bad guys in a game is one thing. Being the short person in the middle of a fight in a small kitchen is another.

"Easy you two," Rita warns.

Mom just stands there, hands on hips, glaring at my uncle.

Stephen opens his mouth to say something but then he squishes up his face, hikes a leg, and farts, long and loud. There's a second between sound and stink but then it rolls over me like a toxic purple cloud.

"Eat this," he grins.

"You stupid idiot," Rita says grabbing her nose and moving fast toward the door.

"Juvenile," Mom tells him. "No wonder your girls are a problem."

Mary Beth joins in. She didn't see the earlier part.

"God, Steve," she says and flaps a dishtowel. "Couldn't you wait until you got outside?"

"Nope." With that my uncle leaves, all except for the lingering purple.

"What was that all about?" Mary Beth asks.

"Your husband's a goat, that's what it's about," Rita fumes.

She slaps two dollars on the counter beside me. "That's payment for my last cuss word and an advance on others I'm sure I'll use before this damn thing is over."

I reach for it, but Mom shakes her head "no," so I leave it.

Mom turns on the exhaust over the stove to pull the fart out. I pour the rest of the cereal in the trash since I'm not hungry anymore. She's rubbing her temples again. Do stinky farts cause brain cancer? I do stinky ones sometimes. Did I do one in my sleep, and it got sucked up in her nose and made the cancer worse? How would I know if I did?

I hug her. I don't care that I'm eleven now and maybe I shouldn't do baby stuff like this.

She hugs me back, smooths my hair, and gives me a loud smacking kiss on my forehead. It feels good.

Mary Beth has poured herself a big bowl of cereal and a cup of coffee and now she's sitting on the couch eating.

"What do you mean that my husband's a goat?" she asks Rita after a couple bites.

I'm not sure if what her sister said finally reached Mary Beth's brain, or she had to think about it first. It's like there hadn't been a two-minute gap in the conversation.

"I mean he's always rude, farting in the kitchen like that. It's rude, and it's unsanitary."

"I'm sure it was an accident."

"It wasn't," Mom snaps.

"You're always picking on him."

"Because he invites it," Rita says.

"Well, I don't like it, and I won't tolerate it."

"He can always take the ferry back to the mainland," Mom tells her. "It's you who has to be here, not him."

I send a psychic message to Mom. *And take Heather and Sarah Beth with him.*

"Same with the girls," Mom says.

It worked!

"What about Henry? If my girls have to go then so does he."

Snap, backfire.

"Peter has been extremely busy at work getting a big project done. Just getting off for Henry's birthday was hard enough."

"He could stay with his other grandma."

Major backfire.

"And your girls could stay with their dad."

"He's busy, too."

Rita snorts.

"You can just stop with the commentary, Rita," says Mary Beth.

Pause.

That's what they call a break in the battle when I have to stop the game and go to the bathroom. It's what happens the rest of the morning and afternoon. Mom and I stay outside. Mary Beth does her daily prayer thing and reads to Riley Rose. Rita stays in her room with her papers and the door closed.

It's evening before the pause ends.

"Burgers again? I'm getting so tired of them. Every three days when Rita is supposed to cook—burgers, burgers, burgers," Mary Beth complains.

"And you don't even cook them. I do," Stephen adds. "We're supposed to all pull a share of the dinners. I don't see why you can't."

"I told you a thousand times already, I don't cook," Rita says. "If you don't like hamburgers maybe you'd better just leave."

I like burgers, but even I'm getting tired of them. Burgers with chips, carrots, or tomatoes. Potato salad would be good, but Rita doesn't know how to make it and Mom and Mary Beth refuse to help.

"I'm tired of them, too," Sarah Beth whines. "Can't you or Aunt Jen do dinner instead of Aunt Rita?"

"No," Mom and Mary Beth say at the same time.

"Time to eat," Rita sings, putting the ketchup and mustard bottles on the counter.

No one talks at dinner except for Heather. She's blabbing away. I think it's because she can't stand the quiet.

"Listen up," Mary Beth finally announces. "I found a

Scrabble game in the cupboard. Shall we play a game after we clean up?"

CHAPTER TWENTY-FIVE

THEY ASK IF MY COUSINS AND I WANT TO JOIN IN THE game. It looks too much like a spelling test to me, so I don't want to play. Heather does. Sarah Beth is in her room with Riley Rose doing something. I don't know what that is, just that she's still too mad to be in the same room as her sister.

"So, you've decided for sure you don't want to bury Momma's ashes near Daddy?" asks Mary Beth.

"We've decided," says Rita.

"Yes," agrees my mom. "Majority rules on this one. If I remember right, in the west corner of the cemetery there's a rise with old oak trees scattered around. I think Mom would have loved it there. It's so peaceful and scenic. When we get back, I'll check to see if there are any lots available."

"Fine, fine. I guess it's close enough that I can still visit both Daddy and Momma.

"Rita, are you coming out for Memorial Day next year? You've never come before but I think it's only right. Both of you really need to come out and help Stephen and I decorate the graves."

"Yeah," says Stephen. "I've said this before, but the

bulk of taking care of Momma Belle and now maintaining the graves always falls on us."

"We heard you the first million times, Stephen." Rita says.

"We'll make sure we come back next year for Memorial Day," my mom tells them.

"You should, too," Stephen tells Rita.

"I'll check my schedule," Rita responds in a sarcastic voice.

My aunt can do a sarcastic voice really good. As good as my uncle can do a sneer face which is what he's doing now at Rita.

"Yahoo, yellow, Y-E-L-L-O-W," Mom says, arranging her tiles on the Scrabble board. "Takes care of my 'y' and the 'w' is a triple. That makes twenty-one points, count 'em and weep."

They play quietly for a while. The click of wood tiles is the only sound.

"That's not a real word, Stephen," Mom says.

"Is, too. N-I-T-E-L-A-C-H, nitelach. You know, that lock thingy on the door."

"You mean night latch?" That's spelled N-I-G-H-T L-A-T-C-H. Plus, it's two words, not one."

"I don't think that's right, and I don't think it's two words. Nitelatch," he says smushing the words together like they're glued.

"Trust me, it's not," Mom says.

"She's right," Rita agrees. She turns to me, "Henry, look in the closet over there to see if you can spot a dictionary, will you."

I start to tell Mom that she has a dictionary app on her phone then I remember, no service.

I look. No dictionary. There's no dictionary anywhere, I discover after I search the cupboards, the kitchen junk drawer, and the same place Mary Beth found the game.

"Do it your way then," Stephen tells everyone after I say I can't find it, "but I'm still right."

No one talks for a while.

"What is the first thing everyone's gonna do when we can go back home?" Mom asks, adding, "I'm going to an exercise class, see a movie, and go out to eat. Anything but stay at home. How about you, Rita?"

"Christ, I'll probably go into the office to see how many stacks of files have landed on my desk. Then I'm going to pour me a big glass of wine, sink into a hot bathtub of bubbles, and enjoy my quiet apartment."

"Mary Beth?"

"I haven't thought much about it. Probably, go to the store. I'm sure the milk's bad by now. And start in on the laundry."

"Get online with my friends and watch tons of television," says Heather, even though no one asked her.

Click, clack, go the tiles.

"Hey, I didn't hear anyone ask me," says Stephen.

Rita mumbles something, but even with super-wolf ears, I can't hear what she said.

Mom must have because she snickers then coughs to hide it.

"If you wanna know, I'm going straight to the dealership and get me a big-ass Hummer."

"To drive the girls back and forth to school?" Mary Beth asks. She's not as good with the sarcastic voice as Aunt Rita, but good enough that my uncle glares at her.

"What do you mean by that, Missy?" he asks her.

"What I mean is that a van for your *family* should be your priority."

He does an eyeroll but doesn't say anything.

"Mode, M-O-D-E," says Rita, laying out her tiles. "Your turn, brother-in-law."

It takes my uncle a long time. He arranges the tiles in front of him then rearranges them, using a hand to shield them from anyone peeking. He starts to place them on the board, stops, and arranges again.

"You passing?" Mary Beth asks.

"No, I'm still thinking,"

"Careful, don't strain the brain," says Heather.

"Can't you shut your daughter up?" he tells Mary Beth.

My aunt doesn't look happy.

"*Zupa*," Stephen finally says and bangs his tiles down. "Z-U-P-A." It's Spanish for soup.

"What?" Rita asks.

"That's not a word," Mom adds.

He glares around the table.

"The hell it is. Ain't any of you ever learned a foreign language? *Zupa*, it means soup.

"We're only using English. And I'm not sure if *zupa* even means soup," Mary Beth adds.

"How the hell would you know? All you do is sit around all day on your fat ass and watch TV. If you'd look at educational channels instead of the crap you watch, then you'd know."

"Like what you tell everyone you do, you mean. Why don't you just tell the truth? The only things you watch are sports and porn on the Internet."

It's weird to see my aunt talk back to my uncle. Everyone is watching to see what will happen next.

"What in the frick were you doing on my computer? I told you it was for my work stuff. And how the hell did you get ahold of my password?"

Mom and Rita inch their chairs back from the table. I lean over the arm of the couch to get closer. No super-wolf ears needed now.

"*Umm*, Mom, Dad," Heather says.

Sarah Beth comes out of the bedroom holding Riley Rose who has her head buried in her sister's neck.

"You selfish bastard. I don't have your password, dummy. I guessed about the porn. But now I know for sure what you do in the office with your door closed."

Snap, caught.

"If you'd lose a few and fix yourself up I wouldn't have to—"

My aunt doesn't let him finish. Instead, she stands up, snaps shut the game board, and throws it at Stephen. Letter tiles scatter everywhere.

Stephen stands up and starts toward her, fist cocked back like he's going to hit her. My aunt tries to get away but her feet tangle in the chair legs. Mary Beth stumbles right, the chair falls left. The chair hits the floor. My aunt keeps stumbling, arms flapping to regain her balance, and then she goes down, a shoulder banging into the bookcase. *Crash* goes my aunt. Wiggle, wobble goes the bookshelf. A vase slides to the floor and explodes in a million pieces. Books tip off, landing *bumpety-bump* on my aunt.

"No," shouts someone.

Nana Belle's urn tumbles, bounces off Mary Beth, and crashes to the floor. The lid pops off and chunky gray powder spills out. A little puff of ash floats up. I suck in a breath, realize that I am breathing in Nana Belle, and hold it.

There's a long second when there's no noise, no movement.

Then there's a howl like a dying wolf in the woods and everything starts up again.

Mary Beth keeps on keening. Mom and Rita rush to help her. Stephen stomps outside, slamming the deck door behind him. I hold my breath, my cousins freeze, and Riley Rose cries for her mom.

Quickly, I run to the bathroom and blow into a tissue, trying to get Nana Belle out of my nose.

When I come out of the bathroom, Mom and Rita are quietly sweeping up my nana's ashes. I don't know where everyone else is.

CHAPTER TWENTY-SIX

I can't sleep. My cousins talk softly in their bedroom. Every once in a while, I hear a word or Riley Rose's high voice, but I don't know what they're saying. Mom is in the living room with my aunties. They're talking, too.

I'm all alone.

"Mom?" I say, opening the bedroom door.

"Go back to bed, honey," she says. "I'll be there in a minute."

It was more than a minute. I fall asleep waiting.

Something is different when I wake up. Bright daylight is coming in the window. Weird, usually I'm awake before then. Then I get it. No *grind, crunch* of the blender. Like bubbles popping, I remember what happened last night: Scrabble, my aunt and uncle fighting, Nana Belle's ashes spilling out, trying not to breathe, falling asleep all alone.

Uncle Stephen is rolling his suitcase across the great room floor when I go searching for breakfast. His hair is all wonky, and his face is blotchy and stubbly. He puts the suitcase by the door then goes back to his room.

Rita is drinking coffee, day twenty-three already

crossed through on the calendar. She looks happy, which is weird, too.

"He slept outside," she whispers to me. "I don't think the night air suits him."

My uncle comes out of the bedroom again, this time carrying a smaller bag. He stacks it on top of the suitcase and takes them outside to the deck.

"Is he leaving?" I ask.

"Yep, he went down to the dock earlier to put the flag up so the ferry will stop."

No wonder my aunt seems happier. Me, too.

Heather and Sarah Beth's door is still closed. I take a breath, ready to ask, but Rita answers before I do.

"The girls are staying; only Stephen is going."

Fiery dragon breath blows all the way out of my lungs.

Everyone moves through the morning like they took slow pills. Stephen stays outside. Mary Beth fixes egg sandwiches and then she and Riley disappear behind her closed bedroom door. Mom and Rita straighten the house up and find a new place for Nana's ashes on top of the fridge. The monster cousins wake up.

"Where in the hell did my Hummer brochure go?" asks Stephen, stomping back inside.

"Don't know," Rita says.

I shrug.

"I think I saw Mom take it," Sarah Beth says. "It'd be cool if we had a Hummer, huh?" she half whispers to her sister.

Heather rolls her eyes and makes a *Pshht,* sound.

"I'm just saying,"

The ferry toots its horn.

Stephen tells Heather, "Go see if your mom has my brochure, quick."

"You do it," Heather hisses.

Stephen looks at the bedroom door, at Heather who stares right back, and at Sarah Beth who is looking everywhere but at her dad.

The ferry toots its horn again.

"Forget it," he says. "I can always get another one from the dealer."

No one walks down to the dock with Stephen to see him off.

The slow pills wear off after my uncle leaves. Kind of. Mom and I swim. She makes me read some out of one of the books she brought, and I have to clean my room. Very boring. Even the ocean looks bored, the waves are flat and slow.

The only interesting part comes when Mr. Taggart walks out of the jungle.

"Ahoy, beach mates," he calls.

"Ahoy, back," Mom answers.

"Thought I'd better let you know there's a storm brewing up south of us," he tells us after they talk about other stuff for a while.

Mr. Taggart stops talking, scans the area. "Stephen around?"

We all look at Mary Beth, waiting for her to say something. She just clamps her lips together.

"He caught the ferry out this morning," Rita finally tells him.

"Oh?"

My aunt still has her lips clamped. It looks like she's afraid if she opens her mouth bad words will jump out.

"Yes," Mom says, nods. "He has business he had to take care of back home in Nebraska."

My aunt's face is red. I think it's because she knows the business involves a visit to a car dealer.

"So, it's just the womenfolk here then?"

Hello. I raise my hand high.

"And Henry. Sorry, son. You're a great helper."

"How did you hear about the storm?" Rita asks. She's still hopeful about phone service but I remember Mrs. Taggart saying that's why they like the island, no phone or television.

"I have a shortwave radio. It'll spit out a warning when one is needed."

"You got a warning?" Mom asks.

Mr. Taggart takes off his hat and scratches his head.

"Not so much a warning, that would mean a storm was imminent. It was a hurricane advisory that there's a storm brewing southeast of here. Sometimes they blow up into something serious, other times they veer away from the mainland. Hard to tell yet."

All eyes focus on him.

"What I'm trying to say is that it's a good idea to monitor the situation."

"You'll let us know if the storm comes closer?" Mom again.

Mr. Taggart shakes his head. "We're closing the house up and leaving tomorrow. This is our summer home. Normally, we've gone back home by now. We winter outside Nashville, but since Alex was here to help do some things, we stayed longer. How much longer you folks planning to stay?"

Rita counts the days out on her fingers. Eight, counting today. I knew that already. But before I can say anything or Rita finishes counting, Mary Beth blurts, "Seven days. We have to stay through thirty days so that makes seven to go after today."

Mr. Taggart raises his eyebrows in a question.

Rita jumps in.

"That's when the lease my mom signed is up."

No mention of Nana Belle's lottery win, or her death, or the will that says we have to stay scrunched together for thirty days, or that Nana didn't really know how long she planned to stay.

"I see," Mr. Taggart says, eyebrows still up a bit. "Looks like we'll leave ahead of you. You let me know if you all need any help boarding up the house, hear? You can close up the shutters to protect the windows."

"Thanks, we will. And I appreciate you letting us know about the storm."

"No problem. I'll let you know if I hear anything more before we leave."

He squeezes my shoulder. "Looks like you're the man of the house now, Henry."

I never thought about it that way. It makes me happy, more so when Heather narrow-eyes me like the funk girl she is.

It's Mom's turn to cook dinner. Burritos wrapped and toasted on the grill and then covered with tomatoes, guacamole, and sour cream. Yummy.

No Scrabble or dominos tonight. I'm glad about that.

Mary Beth is in the kitchen talking to no one. "Night, Momma, and sorry for all the upset." She kisses her fingers and reaches high on top of the fridge to press the kiss onto Nana's urn.

We all go to bed early. I brush my teeth—beating my cousins to the bathroom-*yeah*-pull the covers up and *zonk*, I'm asleep.

For a while, anyway. I'm dreaming Uncle Stephen is coming back, the door to the deck opening with a creak. Then I'm awake, realizing the creaking is real. My uncle is back? That can't be right since the ferry doesn't run at night.

I wonder if I should wake up Mom, but then remember Mr. Taggart telling me I'm the man of the house.

I'm not so happy about that now.

Real quietly, I open the bedroom door a crack. No movement in the dark great room that I can see. Like a panther, I pad-pad to the deck door and find it partially open. Did I see someone lock it before we went to bed? I can't remember. Gulp. Thumpity, thump, goes my heart. Slowly, slowly I squish my face into the gap in the door and look: right, up, down, left. Ghost to the left! I yank my head back in, nearly scraping off an ear. Freak, frack, frock. I'm gonna puke.

I don't puke. After a minute, my heart slows, and I can breathe again. I touch my ear to make sure it's still attached and not bleeding. That's when I realize the door is still open…AND THE GHOST IS OUTSIDE.

I wish my dad was here. I wish Stephen was here. I don't want to be the houseman.

Then the ghost flits in front of the door. It's a short ghost. That's better but still, it's a ghost. Wait. No. Not a ghost. I pull the door the rest of the way open.

CHAPTER TWENTY-SEVEN

"RILEY ROSE, WHAT ARE YOU DOING OUTSIDE?" I DON'T tell her that she scared me so much I almost puked.

"'Enry, come quick. Kitty outside."

The kitty thing, again? I can't believe it.

"You need to come inside before—" I almost said before the ghost gets you, but I stop before I say it.

I reach out to pull Riley inside, but she bounces out of my way.

"I show you," she says. "Kitty drinking milk."

I take a step toward her but again she bounces away.

Dragon poop.

"Okay, Riley, I'll look but we need to be quick before, before…before your mom knows you're outside."

She pulls me toward the stairs. Then she squeals and really bounces.

"Look, look."

She points out toward the water, and I see a shape running away from the house and toward the forest.

Snap, there really is a cat. At least it runs like a cat, fluid and fast. Too small to be a panther, but could it be a baby one? Probably not. I can see the flash of four white paws as it runs.

"Two," Riley says. She's moved to the top of the stairs and is pointing down.

Okay, I'm a believer. If there is one cat there could be two. I follow her, the half-moon partially illuminating the dark steps. One step down, two. Riley is a couple of steps below me.

"See," she says pointing to the bottom of the stairs.

I see something move across the step like it has finished the milk and is now moving away. It is the size of a cat and black with a—oh crapola, hold it. As it moves from dark to less dark, I see a white stripe running from head to tail.

"Ahh, Riley," I say, reaching down to pull her back up the steps.

She turns toward me. I'm moving backward up the steps pulling Riley along. Riley is shouting, "no, no" and trying to pull away from me.

Kitty hikes up a tail and—there she blows.

Skunk stink rolls up the steps and *whack, bam* catches us before we can reach the top.

Riley coughs. I gag. A light comes on in Mary Beth's room.

CHAPTER TWENTY-EIGHT

"I KNOW THERE'S TOMATO JUICE IN HERE SOMEWHERE," yells Mom, her head in the pantry.

"Here," Rita says, coming out from under the island with a bottle in her hand.

I watch all this from outside where Riley and I have been banished.

"Don't just stand there," Mary Beth tells us. "Strip off those PJs. Now."

She's already stripping the nightgown off Riley, her hands in a pair of yellow dishwashing gloves.

Heather and Sarah Beth are watching the strip show from the door, noses pinched with fingers. Bad enough they see me take off my PJ's, no way I'm losing my underwear while they're watching.

"Oh, God, that's awful," says Rita handing out the bottle of juice and quickly closing the door.

Mom brings towels and dish soap. "Down to the shower," she commands.

Really? Past where the skunk spewed?

"Can't I just..."

"Down," orders Mary Beth, "and don't step on any skunk gunk."

Thirty minutes later and I'm back inside, scrubbed pink, and freezing in clean PJs. And clean underwear. So is Riley who has been crying ever since we got sprayed.

"What were you thinking, huh?" This Mary Beth says to me. "A skunk. Some kitty that turned out to be."

I start to explain that it wasn't my fault, that I was just trying to get Riley back inside but Riley's still crying and looking so upset I just shrug and say, "Sorry."

Mary Beth turns to my mom and asks, "What was he doing out there, anyway?"

Mom knows what really happened. I told her as she poured tomato juice over me and rubbed it through my hair.

"You shouldn't put this solely on my son," she says right back.

"Riley's just a baby. Your son shouldn't have taken her out there. Who knows what could have happened?"

"Like running into a skunk?" snarks Rita.

Mary Beth whirls and jabs a finger at her sister. "Exactly like that. Or something worse, like drowning. We would have never found my baby."

"You ever think that maybe Henry was the one who tried to rescue Riley?"

Go Mom.

"My daughter would not have gone out there by herself. Why the hell would she do that anyway in the middle of the night, tell me that?"

"You mean like looking for her cat?" Rita points out.

Mary Beth stops talking. She stares at Rita, at Mom, at me, and then at Riley Rose, still sniffing a little.

No one says anything. I can't stand the silence.

"I think there really is a kitty," I admit. "I saw something like a cat with white paws running away, right before the skunk."

My little cousin gives me such a big smile that I almost forget my arms still sting from all the juice and scrubbing.

CHAPTER TWENTY-NINE

"Hᴏᴛ ᴅᴀᴍɴ, sɪx ᴅᴀʏs ʟᴇғᴛ, ᴀɴᴅ ᴛʜᴇɴ ᴡᴇ ᴄᴀɴ ʟᴇᴀᴠᴇ this place," says Rita, marking through the calendar date.

She takes a dollar out of her pocket and smacks it down on the table where I'm eating breakfast; waffles this morning.

"Two quarters for the cuss jar, and the rest is credit."

I scoop up another bite of waffle, but I leave the dollar where it landed. Mom nods to me, picks up the dollar, and stuffs it into the liter soda bottle we're using as the cuss jar since we already filled up the coffee cup.

"Praise God, homeward bound soon," says Mary Beth and makes the sign of the cross.

"It'll be good to get back to normal." Mom sighs. "I miss Peter, and I miss not being able to jump into the car and go somewhere, even if it is just to the grocer."

"I miss my friends," Heather says, forking a couple of waffles onto her plate.

"Me, too," says Sarah Beth.

"How about you, Rita?" Mom asks.

"I'm with you on the getting out of here. I'm looking forward to restaurants and a movie or two. That's my secret pleasure, watching a movie in the middle of a weekday afternoon. Heck, I don't even know what's playing anymore. Sis, how about you?"

"My big, soft, king bed," Mary Beth says and rubs her butt. "That mattress, I swear, is a hand-me-down from a Girl Scout camp."

Everyone turns to look at me.

"Riding my bike. And seeing Dad again."

"Yeah, I can't wait to see my dad, too," Sarah Beth adds. "And ride in Dad's new Hummer. I hope he gets a red one. Red is my favorite color. After pink."

Everyone turns from me to Sarah Beth. Rita snorts.

"I mean if it's okay with Mom. Dad getting a Hummer, I mean."

Awkward.

"And what about that Hummer?" Rita asks Mary Beth. "You going to give Stephen the money for it? Me, I'd tell him he could just earn it himself; the big shot, real estate tycoon."

My aunt does that air quote mark thingy when she says real estate tycoon.

"He is my husband, so the money is half his, right?"

"Nope. Inheritance is not part of jointly owned property," Rita says. She narrows her eyes like she's thinking hard. "I suggest you do a couple things when you get back home. First, keep the funds in an account just in your name, don't co-mingle it with Stephen's. Second, you really need to consult with an attorney to make sure Mr. Greedy can't stake a claim on Mom's money. A postnuptial agreement they call it."

"That makes it sound like a divorce."

"It sounds like protecting your interests. Today, the expensive Hummer. Tomorrow, who knows what."

"We're a Christian family. I'm not getting a divorce."

"Suit yourself, then. Don't come crying to me after he's spent all the money and you have to go back to work."

"I don't see that happening," Mom says. "There's a lot of money—millions each."

Rita does the snorting thing again.

"You'd think so, but believe me, I've seen a lot practicing law. A married couple starts arguing, and pretty soon, wifey goes shopping in a snit, and boom she drops a few thousand on clothes. Then hubby gets revenge by buying a boat. Wifey takes a trip to Paris. Hubby takes on an expensive blonde girlfriend. They end up divorced and bankrupt. Only winner is blondie, who has maxed out the hubby's credit cards."

My aunt winds up, ready to shoot back. Time for me to bolt.

I have a plan this morning. It rained last evening but had stopped before Riley and I got skunk bombed. Cowboy movies are my dad's favorite. Cowboys can track the bad guys, or wild animals, by looking for footprints in the dirt. I go down the stairs, jumping the last two steps since it's still a little stinky near the bottom where the skunk was. That smell is going to be stuck in my nose for a long time.

Yippee, (that's what they say in cowboy movies) there are prints around the bottom of the stairs. The milk is gone, which explains why there are so many. One set of tracks angles toward the beach. Another line goes around the corner of the house and then takes off toward the trees.

I squat and examine one set of tracks, then the other. They look different. The ones that go around the house toward the trees look longer, like creepy little hands with fingers and claws. The prints that angle toward the beach are rounder and I don't see claw marks.

I think about this for a while. I wish we had Internet so I could Google skunk and cat prints. I know cats can pull the claws inside their toes. Do skunks?

"Mom," I say, pulling open the door. "Look what I found."

First, she has to put the breakfast dishes in the dishwasher. Then she has to wipe off the table. Next, the syrup bottle has to be wiped down and put back in the cupboard. Finally, finally, she's done. All the bouncing and telling her to hurry has just made her move slower.

By the time we go back outside, the sun has dried the prints and sand has crumbled around the edges. It also doesn't help either that Heather or Sarah walked right through them.

She looks at them for a long time, squatting like I did, so she can see better.

"See what I mean? Cats have claws that go in—there's no scratchy marks on these. The others look different. I saw the skunk go that way."

I didn't really since I was trying to pull Riley up the stairs but since the skunk disappeared it must have run around the house. Right?

The one that ran toward the beach must have really been a cat because I have never seen a picture of a skunk with white paws.

"I don't know, Henry. The prints lost their shape when they dried. They kind of look different but I can't say for sure."

Aghh! She should have come right away so she could see what I saw. I don't say that out loud.

———

"Whew, did you forget to put on deodorant?" This from Heather, the queen of rude. I'm leaning over the deck rail, binoculars to my eyes. It was the three-thousandth time, at least, that I'd heard Heather and Sarah Beth make a smelly joke about me today. I ignore her.

I'm panning between the ocean and forest looking

for pirate ships, or a black animal with four white paws, when Mr. Taggart walks out of the forest. He looks really close through the binocs and he's carrying two red, plastic fuel cans.

"Ahoy," says Sarah Beth and giggles.

My cousin, the bright one. Not.

"Ahoy, back," Mr. Taggart answers.

"Are you sure we're going to need this?" Rita asks after Mr. Taggart explains the gasoline is for a generator.

"I don't recall ever seeing one," Mom says, looking puzzled.

"I'll show you," he says. "Maybe you'll need it, maybe not, but best be ready. I heard on the shortwave that the storm in the south Atlantic is intensifying and getting closer. They're not calling it a hurricane yet, but those tropical storms can turn in a couple of hours."

"It's coming our way, then?" Mom asks.

"Hard to tell where and when it'll make land. Right now, they're predicting a broad landing point somewhere between northern Florida and here. Won't be able to narrow the track down until it gets closer. My wife and I already planned to leave this afternoon, but I'm concerned about you folks."

"So, you're thinking we might be in danger?" Rita asks.

"Well, I've lived in hurricane country for many a year, and I would bet by tomorrow the tropical storm will have become a hurricane and acquired a name. Whether you're in danger depends on how strong the thing is and where it's going to come ashore."

"You mean like living in Nebraska long enough to feel when a storm is gonna brew up a tornado," Mary Beth adds as she joins us on the porch with Riley.

"Something like that. So, you folks still planning to stay 'till the end of summer, then?"

Mom and my aunts look at each other and I know they're counting the days we have left to stay.

"I guess you'd better show us how to work that generator," Rita finally answers.

Later, I follow Mr. Taggart back to his house, with Mom's permission, of course.

"I appreciate you helping me, Henry," he says as we walk through the forest. "It's not as easy for me anymore to clamber over the boat and fasten the tarp snug. Plus, if I fall my dear wife would kill me. That is if the fall doesn't take me out first."

He laughs. I'm not so sure it's funny. I'd had talked with Mrs. Taggart, and I don't think she's the murdering kind. Mr. Taggart, the jokester.

"I'll boost you aboard," he says after he works the lift to raise the boat out of the water. Then he partially unrolls the tarp and tosses it to me.

"The easiest way to do this is to start aft, that's the back, and work forward. Put those loops on the tarp around these here hooks; see them along the edge? That's good. Stretch them tight and double loop them. Good, keep going. Unroll, hook, and then move forward. Good, good."

I get it done real fast.

"Careful, Henry. Slow down so you won't slip."

He says that when I'm on the front of the boat, after I had unrolled it a little ways, and then got on top of the tarp to roll it out the rest of the way. Since I had taken off my shoes before we started, and my feet are sticking to the tarp, I'm not worried. Plus, there is water underneath and I'm a super good swimmer. When I'm done, I stand and can almost touch the ceiling of the boat shed.

"Thanks, son," Mr. Taggart says after I jump from the boat back onto the dock.

He looks at me all serious like, which I find weird

since we'd been joking as we worked. Then he puts a hand on my shoulder.

"I'm still worried about your family staying. I wish they'd pack up and take the ferry out. You'll lose a few days on the rental, sure, but it'd be better than trying to ride out the storm."

I nod but don't say anything. We're staying because they have to or lose Nana's big lottery money, but I can't explain that to Mr. Taggart.

"Okay, then," he finally sighs.

He takes a key out of the generator, and we wrap the generator up in a tarp using bungee cords to keep it covered.

"See that box up there under the eave?" he asks after we're done.

I can barely make out a dark box thing next to the post.

"There's an extra key for this generator and one for the boat tucked inside. The top of the box slides open. Just be careful not to drop the keys. There's a bobber on the keychain but it's still hard to find them in the water."

He gives me that serious look again. I still don't understand why. He puts a hand on my shoulder and leans down to look me square in the eyes.

"Make sure to remember everything I showed you in case you need…well, in case you need the boat before you leave. Understand?" He looks out at the sea for a while. "Or if you come back next summer."

I nod that I understand. I think he means if the storm comes. Although, coming back next summer would be great but only with Mom, Dad, and me and no one else. Would we come back here again? I didn't know.

I return home, a sack in each hand. One has milk and bread that Mrs. Taggart said would just go bad if we didn't use it. In the other is a container of home-made peanut butter cookies.

"Had to use up the peanut butter and flour before we go," she had said and winked at me.

I'm hungry after helping cover the boat, so four of the cookies disappear on the way home.

CHAPTER THIRTY

"So, what do you two think?" Mom asks as Mary Beth and Rita help her with dinner.

"I think we have one worried old man," Rita says. "I mean, it's a tropical storm that might or might not become a hurricane. Then the experts don't even know where it'll land. There's, what, a thousand miles of shoreline between Florida and here?"

"It pays to be cautious," Mom tells her.

"Have you looked outside? Blue sky with not a cloud as far as we can see."

"I think we should leave. You don't have any kids to worry about, but we do." This from Mary Beth.

"If you and the girls want to leave, go ahead. I'm staying put," Rita says.

Mary Beth puts her fists on her hips. "It's always about the money with you, isn't it? You'd stay even if you had to ride out the storm in the attic."

"I don't think the water will get that high." Mom adds. "I suggest we wait and see. If it looks like it's going to storm, we can always take the ferry out and then come back, right?"

"No, we have to stay here; that's what Mom's will says."

Mary Beth harrumphs. "Like I said, it's all about the money to you. My girls and I could get swept out to sea and you wouldn't even go after us, would you?"

"I'd save you. I'm not that cold-hearted."

"I'll believe that when I see it."

"Everyone, dinner's ready. Stop arguing and let's eat," says Mom.

Dinner is spaghetti and meatballs. Mom makes the best meatballs, all fried crunchy on the outside and juicy in the middle. At home, she makes her own spaghetti sauce, but the one from the jar she used tonight is still good.

Everyone is quiet while we eat, forks busy. When Stephen was here, he always had to talk, talk, talk while we ate. This way is better. No one seems to miss him, especially Rita who I know doesn't miss listening to him buzz his morning health drink. Even Heather and Sarah Beth don't seem too unhappy he left. I miss my dad so much just thinking about him makes me big sad.

"I've been thinking," Mom says after a while. "This house was built, what in the seventies or eighties? I bet it has weathered lots of storms and look, it's still standing. If the house has survived this long without being blown away, I'm sure it can handle whatever might be coming."

"Good point," Rita agrees, stabbing another meatball out of the bowl. "Have you noticed those shutters aren't just for show? If the weather gets bad, we can fasten them over the windows and doors and just ride it out."

"I still don't think...," Mary Beth says, but then she stops, looks at Rita and Mom. She sighs. "Alright, if you all are staying, looks like I have to, too. God only knows what expensive boy-toys my husband has ordered."

Rita spears a bite of meatball with her fork and then

points the fork—meatball and all—at her sister. "You need to learn how to stand up to that man."

"Like you would know, Ms. Hot Shot Attorney with no family responsibilities."

"I know enough to recognize a damn bully."

"Shut up, both of you," Mom tells them. "Rita, what would happen if we all left until the storm threat is over and then come back. Does that count?"

"Depends on what the will says." Rita.

"Where is Mom's will, anyway?" Mary Beth asks her. "The attorney gave you the only copy."

My auntie shrugs. She looks unsure, not like Rita at all. "That's the question isn't it?"

Mary Beth frowns. "What do you mean by that?"

"We were busy with Mom passing away and us in a hurry to get out here. With all the packing and shopping I must have misplaced it somewhere."

"You lost the will?" Mom exclaims.

"How could you?" Mary Beth whines.

"Just great," Heather mutters.

"It's not lost, I'm telling you. Just misplaced somewhere."

"Did you leave it back in the motel?" Mom asks.

"I don't think so. I remember sticking it somewhere in my luggage or briefcase, or a box, but I can't remember where."

"No money?" asks Heather.

"No Hummer?" Sarah Beth says.

"No, No. We're alright. Old Mr. Daniels, Mom's attorney, has the original. He's supposed to file it in probate court. They'll have a copy, too."

"Like I trust him not to lose it," Mary Beth groans.

Mom's rubbing her head again. It's the first time she's done it since my uncle left. So much for hoping for a miracle cancer cure. If a headache comes and goes does that mean it's something other than cancer? The talk about the will makes me remember that I want to ask Mom if I can get a puppy when I get back. How much does a puppy cost? More than a video game? Mom's still talking so I guess I'll wait to ask about the puppy.

No dominos again tonight and nobody wants to play Scrabble after the fight between my uncle and aunt. I'm reading my book for about the millionth time since Mom said "no" to playing video games after supper. I hate to admit it, but I'm kind of bored with playing games, anyway. Not that I'd ever say it out loud.

Mary Beth is talking to Nana's urn on top of the fridge. "What do you think, Mama? Leave or stay? Is there going to be a hurricane or just a little rain?"

Creepyola, like she expects my nana to answer.

"Twilight Zone," Rita says, real soft.

Mom covers her mouth, but her eyes are laughing.

"Those ashes in there going to tap once for "yes" and twice for "no"?"

"Don't make fun, Rita. I know Mom's spirit is still here because I feel it. Every night I pray for guidance."

"And what does our dearly departed mother tell you?"

"She'll send a sign when she's ready."

I'm thinking about the night when the urn did a wobble, wibble, fell off the shelf, and the cloud of ash dust that spilled out. I think everyone is thinking the same thing about that possibly being a sign because no one talks for a long time.

"I'm heading to bed," Mom finally says.

I lie in bed with the window open, listening for changes in the surf as it swishes in and out.

Sleep.

Awake.

Someone is screaming. Sarah Beth? Not again. Footsteps and doors opening. Not Sarah Beth or Heather.

"There's something outside," Mary Beth shouts, pointing toward her bedroom. She's dressed in one of those old-timey, long nightshirts. She trembles, making everything underneath the nightgown jiggle. She folds her hands over her heart. "Oh, Lord, it's Momma's spirit. What are you trying to tell me, Momma?"

Now this is creepy.

Outside her bedroom window, four white orbs move across the screen when we go look. There's a scratching noise as they shift, left and right, up and down. A dark face with big glowing eyes appears. I see…

Meow

Whiskers.

"Holy crap," exclaims Rita.

"Oh my God," cries Mom.

"Momma?" asks Mary Beth.

"Kitty wants milk," Riley declares.

Heather and Sarah Beth sleep through it all and totally miss it.

"Where do you think it came from?" asks Mom after they get the cat inside. "It's a pretty little thing, all black with the white blaze on its face and mitten feet."

Between a bowl of milk and Riley calling "kitty, kitty," we had managed to catch it. Now full of milk, the cat is licking its paws.

"I'm just glad it's not the skunk," says Rita.

Done grooming, kitty curls up on a very happy Riley's lap.

The cat-cushion cousin giggles. "Tickles."

"That's your kitty purring," explains her mom.

My mom smiles. "It looks like you're going home with a new family member."

"No way. Stephen hates cats. Dogs, too, unless they're outside ones."

Mom and Rita give my aunt a look but don't say anything. I'm thinking the look means if my uncle wants a Hummer, then Riley's gonna keep her cat.

Mary Beth turns to Riley, who's petting the kitty and talking baby talk to it. She sighs. "I don't know how we're going to get the thing home. What does it cost anyway, bringing a cat to Nebraska with us on the plane?"

Mom and Rita stay quiet.

Mary Beth looks up at the ceiling, "Oh, Lord, help me. I asked Momma to send me a message and what does she send? A dang cat. What's she trying to tell me, huh?"

"All a mystery to me," says Rita, very mysteriously. "We got anything around here we can use as a cat box? And we don't have any cat litter."

"Sand," I say. Hello, did everyone forget we're on a beach?

"Looks like you're going to need a name for your kitty," Mom tells Riley. She's sitting beside Riley and rubbing the cat's ears. "What about Mittens since she—or is it a he—has four white feet."

"Mittens," answers Riley, nodding hard.

Mom lifts up Mitten's butt and examines it.

What the bonk?

"Make that Ms. Mittens."

Here's my chance. I take a deep breath.

"Mom?" I say, sitting down on the other side and pulling her arm around me.

"What, kiddo?"

"You think I could get a puppy when we go back home?"

They all laugh, even though I don't think it is funny.

"How can you resist those puppy dog eyes?" adds Rita, laughing.

I still don't see what's so funny.

Mom gives me a hug. "Let me talk to your dad about it first but, yes, there just may be a puppy in your future. We'll call it a late birthday present."

Yippee.

Heather and Sarah Beth are still sleeping, totally missing everything.

Two yippees.

CHAPTER THIRTY-TWO

TOOT, TOOT, GOES THE FERRY'S HORN THE NEXT morning.

"Good, he's brought our supplies," Mom says.

Rita slips on her sandals. "Last load. This should hold us the few days we have left."

We all go down except for Mary Beth and Riley. And Mittens.

Heather and Sarah Beth are pouting since they slept through the cat excitement last night. This makes me happy.

"There's a big storm brewing off the coast," the ferry captain announces when we walk down to the dock. "Hurricane Adele, they're calling it. Weather bureau is telling people they need to evacuate the islands and low-lying areas."

"We've decided to stay," Rita says. "This old house has weathered storms before, and we have a generator. We'll be fine."

He shakes his head and says something low. Midwesterner, I think. "You're from Nebraska, right? At least the old lady that was staying here told me so. I suppose you folks are the fools who go outside with cameras when a tornado blows through. I'm gonna go on down the coast then do a turn 'round and come back before three this afternoon. If you change your mind, run up the flag and I'll stop and pick you up. Okay?"

"Will do," Mom says. She doesn't sound as certain as Rita.

The day feels heavy as we bring the supplies and mail back up the hill to the house. Even the ocean looks flat and gray.

Rita says, "I still don't see any clouds. Weather forecasters in Chicago, they're always warning of some storm or other, and then it turns out to be nothing."

"I don't know," Mom says. "See how dark the horizon is, especially to the south." She points out to sea, where there's a wide dark rim above the water.

"*Pssst.*" Rita exclaims.

"Why don't you stand outside and watch," Heather tells me. "When you blow away, we'll know the hurricane is here."

"Yeah," says Sarah Beth.

I hate my cousins.

Mary Beth is cooking big time when we get back.

"Oh, good, you got the shortening. I'm frying up chicken and making cookies. That way if the power goes off, we won't starve."

Rita looks her sister up and down. "I doubt we'll starve to death in a couple of days. We have deli meats and bread for sandwiches and there's leftovers in the fridge."

"Well, I'm cooking anyway. All this makes me nervous, and when I'm nervous I have to bake cookies."

"Chocolate chip," says Heather.

"Snickerdoodles," adds Sarah Beth.

I'm good with both, growls my tummy.

We spend the rest of the morning closing and latching the hurricane shutters. I can't believe the spiders we find hiding behind them. Seeing them makes my cousins squeal like piggies. Funny. We're all working outside except for Mary Beth and Riley. My aunt is busy scooping spoonfuls of dough onto pans and then sliding the baked cookies onto waxed paper. It makes the house smell great, and we have to stop a couple times to sample them. Yum.

Riley is busy making a bed for Mittens. Finally, we're done except for the big roll-down shutters that cover the sliding door to the deck.

"We need a way to see what's happening outside," explains Mom. "At least until the storm arrives."

"Fine with me," Rita says. "Too claustrophobic in here, anyway."

The wind is blowing hard by the time we finish, and there are dark clouds as gray and swirly as the ocean.

"It's almost two-thirty," Mary Beth says. "You said the ferry was coming back by around 3:00. We can still change our mind and put out the flag."

We all think about that for a while.

"I'm thinking it hinges on what's in Mom's will," Mom says.

"You ever find that thing, Rita?" asks Mary Beth.

"Right now. I'm looking right now." Rita disappears into her room and slams the door.

"What do you think?" Mom asks Mary Beth.

"I'm going to pray on it."

"Better pray fast. We're running out of time."

"We leaving, Mom? I thought we decided to stay?" Heather asks.

Mary Beth has her hands clasped together, head raised, mumbling something.

"Hey, Mom," Heather is louder this time.

"I'm packing," says Sarah Beth, turning for her room.

"Hello, Mom. Quit praying and answer me," Heather badgers.

Heather is a lot like her dad, I'm thinking. I want to stay since I've never been inside a hurricane or a tornado. I'm eleven now, I need experiences. It'd be fun telling my friends all about it.

I really, really wish Dad was here.

Heather tugs her mom's arm. "Mom, I need to know now. I have to wash my hair and get ready if we're going."

Like that would help.

There's a big gust of wind, and I hear raindrops splat on the tin roof.

"Too late, now," declares Mom.

"Jesus, wrap your powerful arms around us and protect us," says Mary Beth, making the sign of the cross, even though she's supposed to be Methodist.

"You're a brat," Heather tells me.

Really? Like what did I do to deserve that? I give her a loud raspberry.

Heather raspberries me back. Sarah Beth does the same. She's always the one for originality, right?

"I'm gonna take a shower," Heather says.

"Me, too," Sarah Beth parrots.

"Holy crapola," Mom says. "Look at those waves."

I'm busy looking, too, so I don't remind her she owes the cuss jar. The waves are big, and the wind is blowing off the tops before they crest. Then it starts to rain harder, the roof drumming.

Mom pounds on Rita's bedroom door. "Rita, come help me roll down the door shutter,"

"Found it," my aunt says when she comes out. She's waving some papers. "It was under my work stuff in a box."

"Too late now. Just help me close up the house."

It's scary watching my aunt and Mom out in the

wind rolling down the door cover. I stay on guard in case I need to help. They duck inside and pull it the rest of the way down.

"I scared, Mommy," Riley cries. She's holding the cat around its stomach, feet sticking out. Mitten doesn't seem to mind. I guess getting squished inside is better than being outside in the storm.

"Damn, that was bad," Rita says after she and Mom come inside. Water is dripping off them. The house is like a cave now, even with all the lights on.

"I'm starving," proclaims Mary Beth. "I'm fixing something to eat. Where did the girls go?"

"They're taking a shower," I answer.

"Good God, with this weather. What happens if lightning hits?"

I entertain this for a moment.

Mary Beth shouts, "Girls, get out here now. Henry, go tell Heather and Sarah Beth to get out of the shower before they get hit by lightning."

"No way."

"I'll do it," says Mom.

Boom goes the thunder, making the shutters rattle.

Screams echo from the girls' room.

Their mom waddles as fast as she can toward their bedroom.

Heather and Sarah Beth burst out still dressed in what they had on before.

"Oh, thank you, Jesus. I thought the lightning done got you."

"We had to get our stuff ready, first." Heather gives me a stink eye. "Since he," she points at my nose, "won't let us keep any of our stuff in the bathroom."

Really? Like it's my fault lightning didn't blast them out of the shower.

"Maybe you'd better thank Henry for that since it's

possible the lightning might have run down the plumbing and electrocuted you."

Go Mom.

"Not," snarls Heather. "Excuse me," she spread out the words real snotty spoiled. "I'm going to take my shower now."

"No, you aren't," shouts her mom.

The house rattles with a big gust of wind and the lights flicker. Everyone stops talking. I hold my breath until the lights even out.

"Fine. I'll just do a sponge bath. Come on, Sarah Beth."

"We should have gone, we should have gone, we should have gone," Mary Beth chants. She's placing cookies in containers, the layers separated with waxed paper. Every time she finishes a layer, she eats a cookie. I'm just hoping the cookies last until the storm ends.

"Like we have any control over the weather," says Rita.

"Well, if you hadn't lost the will, we could have left before all this started," Mary Beth mumbles.

"It wouldn't have made any difference, don't you see. I can't control the weather, and I can't control Mom's misguided effort to keep us together. Damn her harebrained lawyer. A month, heck, it's felt like a year."

"What does Mom's will say about emergencies like this?" my mom asks.

"Well, if you two stop blabbering on, I could read it."

"Anyone want some fried chicken?" Mary Beth asks. "I'm fixing me some."

"I do, I do," I say.

"Good God, Sis, you just ate a dozen cookies. No way you could be hungry," Rita says, still reading.

"I can't help it. I eat when I get nervous."

"You must be nervous a lot then."

Mary Beth laser shoots Rita with her eyes. "That's

mean, Rita. Just because you're a tight bag of bones doesn't mean you have a right to criticize."

Rita gives her sister a long look. About the time I'm thinking a war is going to start up, my auntie surprises me.

"Sorry, Sis. Shouldn't have said that. I'm worried about the storm, too."

No one talks for a while. Then Mom asks, "How long do these things last, anyway?"

"Hell, if I know," Rita answers.

"I hungry," Riley Rose says, rubbing her tummy.

"Me, too."

"Good grief." Mom pinches her brow again.

CHAPTER THIRTY-THREE

I'M EATING A CHICKEN LEG WHEN THE LIGHTS GO OUT. We wait, but they don't go back on. I hear banging. It's Mom stumbling around.

"Ouch! Crap, where did those candles go?"

Something glows.

"Here, use this," says Rita.

"You have your cellphone? All this time, it's been in your pocket? I thought we didn't have reception?" declares Mom.

"We don't. I just, well, it's a habit."

"It's still charged? Mine is dead by now."

"I charge it every night."

"Good grief," Mom says.

"Found some," says Mary Beth from under the kitchen island. "Anyone got matches?"

"I have a lighter in my pocket." Rita digs out her lighter, strikes it, and lights one of the candles.

Mom laughs. "You should have been a Girl Scout."

"I was."

"I found flashlights, too," Mary Beth says.

"Generator," I say to Mom.

"Generator," she relays to my aunts.

I so wish my dad was here.

"I guess someone has to go start it," Mary Beth tells us.

"Not me. Me either," That from my cousins, the "brave souls."

"I can," I volunteer.

"No, son. Rita and I will."

"Might as well, I'm still damp from closing the shutters."

Neither of them moves for a minute.

"I wish Dad was here," I say.

"Me, too," agrees Mom.

"My dad, too," says Sarah Beth, and she looks like she's ready to cry.

I'm not going to cry, no matter what.

"Heather, you and Sarah Beth come with us. Stay inside, but if we yell or bang, you open the door."

"I can help," I offer, but no one listens to me.

The generator is attached to the back of the house inside a three-sided shelter with a roof. It's open on one side so the exhaust can go out. The house is shaking badly in the wind, but as I walk down the short hall to the back, it doesn't seem as bad. I guess that's because the storm is attacking us from the sea side, not the back.

It's scary, knowing Mom and my aunt are going outside. We so need Dad. Even Uncle Stephen would be okay for this.

Mom and Rita are wearing yellow slickers they found in the closet. If it wasn't so scary outside, they would look funny like giant rubber duckies.

"Ready?" Rita asks, pulling up her hood.

"Ready," answers Mom, pulling hers up, too.

"Go," they say together to Heather, who has her hands on the doorknob.

Heather opens the door and *blast,* in comes the wind

and rain. Rita and Mom dip their heads, grab each other's hands, and go.

Please, please be careful. I don't want to be an orphan. I don't want to be stuck here all alone with my cousins.

Heather and Sarah Beth push the door shut behind them and put their backs to it.

My heart beeps, beeps, fast. The hallway is dark and wet. That makes it worse. The three of us listen but all I hear is the wind roaring and rain on the roof. It stays dark. I wait forever; time enough for the sun to burn out and the universe to collapse into nothingness.

Bam, bam, bam, on the door.

Heather and Sarah Beth yank the knob and in fall Mom and Rita, soaking wet. Their hoods are off, and water streams off their heads and coats.

"Close the door. Come on, help."

Mom and Rita crawl in so the door can swing shut and Heather, Sarah Beth, and I push and push to close it against the wind. Finally, Heather clicks the deadbolt lock.

"Well, that didn't work like we thought," says Mom, still lying on the floor. She starts to laugh hysterically. Then Rita laughs and we all laugh, covered in rain in the dark hall. Snap, is this crazy to be laughing? It's like listening to a pack of hyenas cackle over a dead wildebeest.

A beam of light hits us.

"Are you alright? What happened out there? It's still dark."

Rita stops laughing long enough to say, "We took a few steps along the wall, then I tripped and pulled Jen down with me."

"And we duck-walked back to the door," says my mom.

More hysterical laughing. It is funny thinking about

them looking like yellow ducks waddling back to the door. Funny now that they are safe inside, of course.

"So, no generator?"

"Didn't even get that far. And no way I'm going to try that again. Right, Sis?"

"Right as rain."

More cackling.

After Mom and Rita are dry again, we stay in the great room, huddled around candles. Heather and Sarah Beth are reading on their Kindles, faces glowing. Mom is eating a sandwich. I'm having snickerdoodles since I already ate chicken and butter bread. Outside it roars like Tyrannosauruses fighting.

"There might have been a way," says Rita, looking up from the papers she's reading.

"What do you mean?" Mary Beth asks.

"To leave the island, Mom's will says we have to stay together for thirty days, right?"

"Right."

"So as long as we're together."

"Yeah, but we were supposed to stay in Mom's old house. Then you said since this was her residence when she died, we could stay here instead. You mean all this time we could have stayed in a nice hotel on the mainland?" Mom asks.

"I can't believe it," Mary Beth adds.

The wind pushes at the house in one direction and then another. The shutters rattle and we all hold our breath for a minute.

Rita continues, "I'm not exactly saying that. I'm saying as I interpreted it, and Stan Daniels agreed, that the spirit of the will was that we stay together at Mom's home and since this was her residence for the last however long of her life, we could just stay here."

"I don't see if that's your interpretation, why we couldn't have stayed in a hotel, back in civilization, instead of out here in nothingville," Mary Beth gripes.

"It's a fine line, I know, but if Mom was residing somewhere, wherever that was when she passed, then we should stay there. What it doesn't say is that we could just willy-nilly stay together anywhere. See the difference?"

Something bangs outside.

"Right now, she's residing on top of the fridge," Mom says.

"That's correct. Now, listen to this. Her will doesn't address what happens if there's an emergency that would cause the residence where we have to stay to be inhabitable or unsafe. For example, if we had stayed at her old house, there was a fire, and the whole thing burned to the foundation. You understand? We can thank that incompetent Daniels for not including an emergency clause."

It all sounds confusing to me, but Mom and my aunt are slowly nodding their heads.

"I'm not sure where you're going with this," says Mary Beth.

"Hear me out. If there is no emergency clause, that gives us room to interpret Mom's intent."

Blank looks all around.

"If an emergency occurs that prevents us from remaining where she lived, then we could interpret her intent to mean we could change locations, as long as—and this is the important part—we reside together."

"So, as long as we keep Momma's urn with us and we stay together, we can keep the money?" Mary Beth asks.

Rita shrugs. "I don't think it requires that Mom's cremains stay with us, but I guess it wouldn't hurt."

Outside the wind is still roaring and rain is beating hard against the house. Heather and Sarah Beth have been listening to my aunt talk, the Kindles no longer lighting their faces. Riley Rose and Mittens are asleep, curled up on the couch beside Mary Beth. I'm still not sure what Rita means, but I'm marking 'lawyer' off my career wish list. It's bonkers confusing.

"The question is," Rita goes on, "whether this," she waves her arm around at the dark room, "meets the definition of uninhabitable or unsafe conditions."

"You mean we could have left before the hurricane came?" Heather asks.

"No, we can't anticipate what might happen, only what does."

"We'd have to take Momma's ashes," says Mary Beth.

"We're leaving?" asks Sarah Beth.

"Again, it depends on what defines an emergency evacuation," Rita points out.

"I want to stay someplace with a McDonald's," Sarah Beth whines.

"I'm not sure the lack of power qualifies this place as uninhabitable," says Mom.

"I think it does," Mary Beth says. "We're in the middle of a stinking hurricane, remember?"

"I agree with Jen," says Rita. "Plus, we have no way to get off the island."

"We're stuck here then?"

"Looks like it."

"No McDonald's?" Sarah Beth asks in the whiny voice.

"Better use that attorney brain and think some more on it," Mary Beth tells Rita. "To me, this place is unsafe."

We all go back to what we were doing before. It seems weird. This is the first time since we came that we're all together in one room. Nobody wants to be alone with the storm, and there's no way we can go outside.

The sound of wind and rain on the roof gets louder. The house shakes when the wind shifts, and the vibrations make my ears feel wonky.

Bang, bang, goes something against the house. It's coming from the side where Mary Beth, Riley, and Rita have their bedrooms. *Slap, bang.*

"One of those damn shutters must have torn loose," shouts Mom.

Bang. The noise repeats a few more times.

Rita sighs. "We'd better go look."

No one moves. Then Rita gets up. She opens her door and looks in the bedroom.

"Fine here."

She opens Riley Rose's door.

"Here, too."

She opens Mary Beth's door.

"Well, shit. We've lost a shutter, and…"

Bang, crash. Tinkle.

"Damn it!"

Rita closes the door fast.

"Something just broke the window. Looks like one of the deck chairs."

"Oh, all my things."

"Not much we can do now."

"My clothes and books will get all wet."

"Later, it's too dangerous now to go in there with the window broken and things flying around outside."

Rattle, rattle goes the door like there's a monster in my auntie's room wanting to get out.

"Forget unsafe. I'd say my bedroom is uninhabitable now. Is that enough for you?"

"It might be, I think."

"Oh, Lordy, think faster. I can't sleep in that bedroom if there's a foot of water in it."

BOOM. CRASH. The loudest one ever. The whole

house shakes like one of those fighting dinosaurs fell on it.

My cousins' bedroom door pops open, and I see green. Everywhere.

CHAPTER THIRTY-FOUR

My cousins scream. Heather and Sarah Beth jump up from the couch and bolt to their mother.

Mitten bolts, too, with Riley racing after her.

I think I screamed, but I'm not sure.

"A tree fell on the house!" yells Mom. She has to yell because the roar is inside now.

"We need to shut that door," Rita shouts back.

I help. Wet leaves, moss, and thick tree branches take up the whole room. We have to push them back out so we can close the bedroom door. Before the door closes, I see, beyond the green, not a wall, but the outside. It's dark, as dark as the inside of the house and I realize the day has gone and it's almost night. We check the bathroom between my cousins' room and mine. There's a crack in the ceiling and water is dripping in, but otherwise, it looks usable. Our room is fine, but Mom and I still put our clothes and stuff into the suitcases and roll them into the great room.

Heather is wailing that she lost everything. Her mom pats her back and tells her they can buy all new stuff when they get home. Sarah Beth has her face buried in her hands, and she's snuffling. Riley is in the kitchen calling for Mittens.

My aunt and Mom are staring at Rita.

"What?"

"This enough for you? No way we can stay here with no electricity. And the girls and my bedrooms are destroyed with water everywhere."

Rita paces the room talking to herself. Finally, she goes into the kitchen, grabs the cookie container, and brings it back. She pulls out a handful of cookies and passes the rest.

"Well?" Mom. "What do you think?"

"I think to hell with my diet."

"Really." Mary Beth says, drawing the word out.

"Yes, really. Here's what I'm thinking. This place is uninhabitable, which voids us having to stay here. As long as we stay together, with Mom," she points to Nana's urn still snuggled on top of the fridge, "that should suffice."

"What if someone protests that leaving here breaks the will?" Mary Beth says.

"Who's going to protest?"

"Well, the lawyer."

"Don't think so. It has to be an interested party with standing to protest the will."

"Speak English," Mary Beth demands.

"It's usually a family member or beneficiary who protests a will. Creditors have standing, too."

"We three are the beneficiaries."

"Yep."

"What about the executor, isn't there an executor? Is it Daniels?"

"Nope, Remember, Mom named the three of us co-executors. Not smart, three executors, especially when, well, we don't usually agree. Not surprised, though, Mom seemed to have had an agenda."

"What about my husband?" asks Mary Beth.

"Stephen may be the lump of coal in your stocking, but he's not a beneficiary. And he has no standing."

"So, you're saying as long as us three agree we're okay?"

Rita points a finger at my mother.

"You got it. We just have to figure out a way to get out of here."

That's when we notice it's quiet—no wind, no pounding of rain.

"Hallelujah, it's over." Mary Beth says, raising up her arms.

"Ah, Mom," Heather says.

"I'm going to see what I can salvage from my room, and we can go."

"Mom." Louder this time.

"I know, I know. Your stuff is gone. You can get new clothes and makeup."

"No, not that. It's the eye. We're in the hurricane's eye. I learned about it in school."

Everyone talks at the same time.

"There's a round two, then?"

"I don't think this house can survive another hit."

"All my things are destroyed."

"Me, too."

"No power."

"Four more days, no way."

"Hey, Mom," I say, shaking her arm.

She says, "The ferry won't come around again until it's all over."

"Mom!" I'm shouting.

"What is it, Henry?"

"Mr. Taggart's boat. We could use his boat. He said it was okay."

Finally, people listen.

"I don't think we can do it, kiddo, but good idea."

"No, Mom. We can. He showed me where the key is

to the boat, and I know how to run the generator that lowers the boat into the water."

Lots more talking.

"It might just work."

"Didn't he tell us they had a shortwave radio?"

"One of us could go, get ahold of the Coast Guard."

"We all have to go together."

"I don't know about this."

"How long does the eye last anyway?"

"If we're going to do it, then we have to go now."

"Pinky swear, we're in this together," Rita says.

Mom and my aunts hook their pinky fingers together, raise their arms and shout, "Pinky swear!"

CHAPTER THIRTY-FIVE

THE CELLPHONES, KINDLES, MY DS PLAYER, AND THE chargers go into sealed plastic bags. We pack a change of clothes in plastic trash sacks, except for Heather and Sarah Beth since a tree takes up their whole room. They complain, but I'm happy. There's not enough room in the boat for all their makeup and junk that I know they would have to bring.

Nana Belle's ashes go inside a sealed food bag, which is wrapped in old newspapers and then tucked inside the plastic container that the cookies were in. Riley finally finds Mittens hiding between the refrigerator and cabinet and the cat is tied inside a pillowcase so she can't see the water. A good thing since she has very sharp claws and runs like Flash Gordon.

We trek through the forest. It's always creepy, but the jungle is worse in the dark. Even with the flashlights, it's hard to tell where the path is since leaves, twigs, and tangles of Spanish moss have covered it.

"Stop for a minute," groans Mary Beth.

She's huffing and puffing, making little moaning sounds when water drips on her. I bet she wishes she was the one doing the health drink and exercising in the morning instead of Stephen.

"We have to keep going," Rita says. "We have no idea when this storm's going to start again."

"The storm is over. Can't you see that?"

"Mom, it's the eye." Heather reminds her.

I agree with her. The air has a crawly, edgy feel. It's like a scary movie when you just know a monster is watching from the bushes ready to pounce. Creepsville.

"We're smacked," says Rita. She beams the flashlight ahead on the path. Except there's no path, just a wall of drippy, slimy green.

We left the cuss jar at the house, so I don't mention the bad word. I'm thinking by the time we get back we're going to owe it bunches. If we ever get back. If we live. What if I never see Dad again? I wipe my eyes, pretending it's just rain on my face. No one notices.

"Too big to go over," Mom tells us. She's been carrying Riley Rose on her back but now she sets her down. Heather has been carrying the pillowcase with a meowing Mitten inside and Riley grabs it when she's on her feet.

"You can help me hold your kitty but I'm not letting go, understand?" Heather tells her.

Mom and Rita examine the tree, pushing branches aside to see.

"We need to go that way," Mom points to the left, "over the trunk is easier than around the crown. We'll be off the path a few feet, but we can make it."

Mary Beth groans.

"Hurry," says Rita.

"Are snakes in there?" asks Sarah Beth looking at the dense, dark wall of trees.

Now is where I'd normally be happy to tell my bratty cousin that there are tons of snakes and crocodiles just waiting to eat them, but they'd refuse to go, and we'd be stuck here when the storm starts again.

Plus, I don't really want to think about things with fangs and sharp teeth hiding in the soggy jungle.

"No snakes," I say. "Come on, follow me."

The mud where the tree's roots were uprooted is slimy. By the time we climb over the trunk and get back on the trail, we're covered with goo.

"This is so gross," says Heather.

We start walking again. Rita is in the lead with the flashlight, then Sarah Beth and Heather with Mittens. Their mom follows them. I'm next. Mom is the caboose carrying Riley Rose.

All the time we walk, I'm trying to remember what I need to do to start the generator and winch the boat down into the water.

Finally, we ooze out of the woods. The Taggarts' house looks worse than ours. The roof is torn off and leaves and moss are stuck to the sides. It makes me sad.

"Rats," says Mom. "I thought when we were walking that maybe we could just stay in their house. Smarter than taking the boat."

"Yeah, but it looks like they have more damage than we do," Rita replies.

"We could see. It might be alright inside," whines Mary Beth. "I've always hated boating. Can't we just look?"

Mom shakes her head. "The doors and windows are boarded up and locked. We could break in, but that takes time, and what happens if we find the house is flooded? There goes our opportunity to take the boat. Henry knows how to get it down. I've driven boats before; Peter and I owned one before we had Henry. Plus, Chuck showed Henry how this setup works. Right, son?"

Gulp.

"I say we go, and quickly," says Rita.

Mary Beth sighs. "All right, all right, let's do it."

I can't remember exactly where the box is with the keys, but finally I see the shape in the beam of the flashlight.

I climb on top of the rail and reach, reach. Mom holds onto my shorts, so I won't fall. My fingers walk to the box. I slide it open just like Mr. Taggart told me, and there are the keys. I hold tight so I don't drop them in the water.

Mom helps me fit the key into the generator, switch on the gas, and turn the key. Everyone, including me, holds our breath. It grinds, and then the motor starts. I press the down switch and the boat lowers to the water. Easy peasy, right? Not. I breathe again. The boat lowers until it floats free in the water.

"Unloop it this way," I tell Heather as she helps take the tarp off the hooks.

I start to push the tarp onto the dock, but Mom tells me to fold it up.

"We may need it to cover ourselves if it starts raining."

I'm thinking if we're hanging onto the corners, the wind is just going to suck us up like being in a tornado, but I don't say it.

Mom checks the boat's fuel and gives my aunts a thumbs-up sign.

Mom, me, my aunts, cousins, Nana's ashes, and one unhappy Mittens board the boat, and Mom starts it.

The motor coughs, coughs again, and then growls to life. Mom checks gauges on the dashboard, moves the throttle forward, and we're off.

Mom shouts, "What do you say, five or six miles to shore?"

Rita shouts back, "Closer to five to where the ferry docks. I say follow the route we took with the ferry around that big island." She points but everything looks black, and I can't see an island. "Then head left between the two smaller islands, under the bridge, and into port."

Mary Beth has her head down, mumbling. Praying, I guess. Heather and Sarah Beth are sitting on the bench seat, Riley between them holding tight to a squirming pillowcase.

Mary Beth raises her head and lifts her hands to the sky. "Thank you, Jesus, for bringing us safely to shore."

A gust of wind pushes the boat sideways.

This must be God humor.

"Not there yet," Rita warns.

"Oh, Lord, keep us close," and my aunt goes back to prayer mumbling.

Mom goes slower than Mr. Taggart did.

I move up beside where Mom and Rita are. They are standing in the yellow raincoats, with feet apart in case the boat rocks again.

"It goes faster, Mom," I say. "Push the throttle up."

"Don't want to, there's debris in the water."

Another gust of wind and I feel raindrops. They splat hard on my head.

"Any life vests on board?" shouts Rita over the noise of the motor.

I nod, remember it's dark and she can't see me, and say, "Yes."

"Get 'em and pass them out. The storm will be on us quick enough."

I'm squatting, pulling them out from under the seats when *Boom, crash,* and I slam to the other side.

Mom shouts bad words.

We do this lurchy thing and then the boat straightens.

"You okay, cuz?" asks Heather.

I put a hand to my head. Blood or rain? I can't tell.

"I'll help you. Come on, Sis."

"No running lights," Rita announces.

"Lost them when we hit something back there. I can't see a freaking thing."

"Down, down," Mary Beth commands, motioning us to sit in the bottom of the boat. Heather and Sarah Beth finish pulling life vests from under the seats. They help each other put them on, then help their mom and Riley. After I get mine on, I scoot two up to Mom and Rita. Rita is hanging over the side shining the flashlight ahead of the boat.

We go so, so slow for a while.

Then the monster in the sky pounces: a sheet of rain slams over us and the wind pushes us left then right.

"There's the two islands," Rita says, "Steer between them, better go, now!"

The boat turns and Mom pushes up the speed a little.

"Don't you dare fall!" Mom is yelling to my aunt who is still bending over the side holding the flashlight so Mom can see.

"Watch out, Mom," I say pointing to something white ahead of us.

She turns the wheel, and everyone watches a big, white cooler float by, looking like a ghost in the black water.

"Gather around, kids," Mary Beth says. She unfolds the tarp and pulls it over them.

"I see lights," Mom shouts and points to them.

Heather's head pops out from under the tarp then Sarah Beth's, their hands holding the tarp tight around their necks. It looks funny like they've hatched from a blue giant's belly. I'm too scared to laugh though because it's raining more, hard drops smacking my head, my back, my face.

Mom and Rita's big yellow rain jackets are flapping, and they keep pulling their hoods around so they can see. I'm kneeling between them, ready to grab my aunt in case she falls in. When I peek over the dashboard, I can see the lights wavering in the rain.

Just when I think we can make it, *BOOM CRASH*, we hit something.

Mom turns the wheel left, then right, her Big Bird arms flapping in the wind.

I hear screams behind me, and I turn to see one side of the tarp fly up in the air. Heather is holding tight, but it's starting to pull her up. My aunt and cousin grab her legs, and she lets go. Up and away flaps the tarp like a giant bird.

"No, no," shouts my aunt.

Nana Belle, inside the urn, wrapped in newspaper, tucked in the plastic cookie container tumbles out of the tarp.

"NOOOO!" someone shouts.

"Momma," someone else says.

It tumbles down and just before we can grab it, the wind blows the container sideways and it's in the water.

Before I can think.

Before I can get scared.

Before Mom can order me to stop, I leap to grab Nana Belle.

I'm in the cold water. Something hits my head and back. I'm under the water. Black everywhere. I can't breathe. I kick my legs as hard as I can, but all around me is dark, and I can't tell what is up or down. Hands grab me, pull me up, and over the side of the boat. I gulp air.

Nana is tight against my chest.

Things are kind of fuzzy after that. I hear Mom, I think it's Mom, screaming my name. The lights are closer, and then the lights are flashing red and blue. I hear deep voices, and someone lifts me up. Things get really fuzzy and then nothing.

CHAPTER THIRTY-SIX

When I wake up, I'm dry. Does that mean clouds are dry in heaven? I move a little, but it makes my back and head hurt. If I hurt, that must mean I didn't die. I open my eyes.

"Decided to join the party, huh?" says Heather. "Hey, everyone, the kid's awake."

I see Mom and my aunties.

And Dad.

Wait a minute. What?

"Dad?" It comes out all croaky.

He hugs me for a long, long time, and I hug him back, real tight.

We all stay in the shelter for the last three days we need to stay together. Dad, I find out later, had been worried and flew out before the storm but missed the last ferry to the island. He had paced, made phone calls, and met each arrival to the shelter looking for us.

We had almost made it to shore when the Coast Guard saw Rita's flashlight and picked us up. The doctors at the hospital checked me out and declared me bruised and a little concussed, but I'd survive. Nana Belle, too, was still safe and dry in the plastic container.

Heather had been the one who fished me out of the

water with Sarah Beth hanging onto one of her legs and Mary Beth the other.

Before Mom, Dad, and I go home, we first fly to Omaha. That's in Nebraska. Mom and my aunties talk to Mr. Daniels while my cousins and I stay in the motel with Dad.

Stephen never comes to see us while we're there, but I know my aunt talks to him a lot on the phone. A couple of times she told Mom and Rita that she needs quiet time and a bottle of wine after she was done talking.

We bury Nana Belle in her urn under a shady tree on a hill in the cemetery. There are other people there at the burial, and they say nice things to Mom and my aunts. I hope Nana is happy in her new home. Can dead people be happy? I'm going to miss her.

I help Heather pick out some good Nintendo games and a controller at the video store. I guess I owe her that for saving me from drowning. We all shop for new clothes and luggage. I don't help Heather with that.

Everyone hugs goodbye at the airport. The hugging seems to go on forever, and they use a ton of Kleenex. I scratch Mittens' ears inside her cat carrier and give Riley Rose a big squeezy hug, but just do a little wave at her big sisters.

When we finally get home, I discover things look both familiar and strange. My bed and dresser look smaller, but Mom says that's just because I've grown.

I get a puppy. His name is Maxwell. He's a golden retriever that sleeps with me every night and chews my socks.

ABOUT THE AUTHOR

Teter Keyes is the pen name used for middle-grade age books written by author Connie L.Beckett. She, and Teter, live in northeast Kansas where Connie is currently working on the next novel.

Other published works include "The Kingmaker and the Scribe," and the Gwen Lindstrom mystery series.

Under the Teter Keyes name, she is also the author of "Lost Lamb, a Deidra Ann Adventure."

———

To learn more about Teter Keyes and discover more Next Chapter authors, visit our website at www.nextchapter.pub.

Nana Belle Wins The Lottery
ISBN: 978-4-82414-528-4
Mass Market

Published by
Next Chapter
2-5-6 SANNO
SANNO BRIDGE
143-0023 Ota-Ku, Tokyo
+818035793528

5th August 2022